The World of Asian Stories

a teaching resource

CATHY SPAGNOLI

illustrations by

Uma Krishnaswamy

Tulika

Although every effort has been made to present correct and current information in the text, I apologise if mistakes have crept in; please write to Tulika Publishers with corrections for the next edition. The maps are not to scale, the borders are approximations, and only a few physical features could be shown, due to space constraints. However, we hope that they give you a sense of the far-reaching Asian world. Use them, as you will the short country introductions, to do more research on your own. A word, too, on the use of italics in the book: the first time a non-English word appears, it is italicised, after which it is not.

I hope that the book, with all its limitations, will inspire you to study further and learn more about this rich and diverse continent. – C. S.

The World of Asian Stories: a teaching resource
ISBN 978-81-8146-354-8
© *text* Cathy Spagnoli
© *illustrations* Tulika Publishers
First published in India, 2007
Reprinted in 2010

Published by
Tulika Publishers, 13 Prithvi Avenue, First Street, Abhiramapuram, Chennai 600 018, India
email tulikabooks@vsnl.com *website* www.tulikabooks.com

Printed and bound by
the ind-com press, 393 Velachery Main Road, Vijayanagar, Velachery, Chennai 600 042, India

For more information about Tulika or to order books visit our website. www.tulikabooks.com

Contents

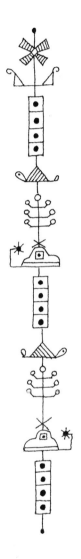

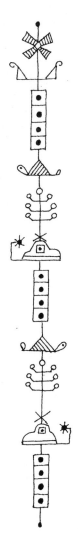

Talking about Telling

Cathy Spagnoli has been collecting stories from all over the world and telling them, particularly in Asia and the U.S.A., for over 20 years. What do stories really do, and what does it actually mean to be a storyteller? Let's ask Cathy.

You belong to a culture that values the rational and the logical, whereas the Asian way is more emotional and intuitive...

Although I was born in the U.S., I belong sort of between cultures! I have roots in the more emotional land of Italy, I have lived in Asia for so long, and I've shared my life with a great man from south India, so I tend to see both sides of this 'balance'. And I think, especially in folklore, we don't see such a difference between rational and emotional; folktales of many nations share certain values that often go beyond such distinctions. There might be more stories of 'larger than life' heroes, like Davy Crockett, Paul Bunyan, etc. in the U.S., but that's only part of our multicultural nation. This is a very big question, and I'd need much more time to truly explore it.

How do you relate to stories that are so different?

From my many experiences in Asia, and my deep friendships in Asia, I don't find these stories so different. In fact, I now know more about Asian folklore and oral literature than I do of Western material (so I have to study that, too!). Over the years, many true stories of my own in Asia have taught me so well about things like Asian hospitality, East Asian social formality, the depth of friendship, the importance of family and respect toward elders, etc. So these values have become a part of our mixed heritage family now!

How successful have you been in communicating this difference to teachers and children in the West? Do they really enjoy stories from such different cultures?

I don't know, truly, how successful I've been, but I have received the nicest notes and emails and comments from those who've read and used my books/tapes, or heard my storytelling programmes. I even get many positive comments from Asians, both in the U.S. and in Asia, who had lost a connection with their own story roots and enjoyed exploring it through my work. And yes, teachers and children in the U.S. and Canada (I haven't really told much in other parts of 'the West') definitely enjoy stories from elsewhere. Teachers there like to explore variants of popular tales across cultures and see how (and why) they differ. They also are eager to know more about how the stories of a culture share some of its values, and they are looking for good stories that do that. Of course, in parts of the U.S. we have people from all over, so it is crucial to understand each other through stories and more.

Does telling stories from other cultures really promote understanding?

A BIG YES. Actually, I think some of the most powerful stories to promote cultural change are the true stories of a culture. Children will often ask after a story, "Did that REALLY happen?" When you say, "Yes", their eyes widen as they pull that truth into their minds. True stories about heroes, both the famous and less known, help understanding, as well as the true stories of daily life and family. My two favourite true stories about India, for example, share Indian hospitality and an Indian sense of family. When I tell either of them, I know from the reactions that listeners are seeing something in a new light, are understanding another worldview, at least a little!

Although I grew up with storytelling – my dad's tales as a journalist, my mom's bedtime fantasies, and stories of the old country and immigration from my Italian relatives, I never thought I'd use storytelling as such a strong part of my work. Then, at the age of 20, I found myself very sick with hepatitis in a general ward in Holy Family Hospital in Delhi. My only friend was a young girl from Afghanistan, for I spoke her language a bit after three months there. But she was very sick and one horrible night I stood by her bed, with her father... She screamed throughout the night. In the morning she looked at her father, squeezed his hand, turned her head, and she was gone. She was my age and my friend. I had so many questions about her death. The next day, a gentle Indian man, sent by my father, a journalist in New York, sat down with a bag of oranges and asked how I was. I said I was fine but pointed to the empty bed asking why? And so began my first deep exposure to stories for he told me stories of Buddhism and Hinduism to try to explain what might happen after death. The stories literally opened doors in my mind.

I returned to Boston, flew through two years of college in one, taught the hearing-impaired and learned sign language, then it was back to Asia for two years. This time I saw so much rich storytelling and worked with Tibetans in the Tibetan School of Drama, Dharamsala, studied dance in Bali, and stayed in a Buddhist monastery in Thailand. From those roots came a strong interest in Asia and a strong passion for storytelling. Back in Boston, I discovered the power of storytelling as a teaching tool in a class. I watched, amazed, as a group of very noisy, energetic young boys were suddenly transformed into silent angels as they listened to the teacher tell 'Abiyoyo', the story of a young boy who tricks a giant.

How do you deal with the danger of making other cultures seem exotic?

You are right, this might happen. But I think it is more of a problem with media such as movies and books, that present visuals that are very 'exotic' and powerful. It is especially a problem when someone hasn't done their cultural research and thus just takes the most 'exciting' story or the one that seems most different, to tell or write. The more one knows a culture, the more stories there are to choose from and the more rounded a cultural picture can emerge.

The stories in this collection have been told the way they probably are in the original, although you contextualise them through the activities and discussions at the end of each section. But doesn't storytelling, by its very nature, imply changing and retelling to suit the time and the audience?

I'm not at all against adapting stories. I just find that as, basically, an outsider to these cultures, I feel most honest using the stories in a fairly authentic version. Of course, I'm working through translations and so my versions may be still quite far from the original. But I hope to provide a foundation for others to work from, especially if they wish to adapt a story. And, remember, although storytelling does adapt itself, many important values remain constant and thus telling some older, traditional stories also remains important.

Yes, there are many stories I would not choose or use because of blatant sexism or terrible violence or very dated ideas. In this book, I tried hard to include a range of Asian voices from past and present, telling in their own ways and words. Think of the book as a basket of story gifts – with copyright and translation challenges, influenced by the time period and setting of the text, and enriched by the views and languages of the writers/tellers.

What are the common motifs, if any, in Asian stories or in their telling?

Asia is huge and varied, so some more common motifs can be found across regions rather than across the entire continent, e.g. Islamic motifs and themes that would be found predominantly in West Asia, and in parts of South and Southeast Asia.
Or Buddhist themes especially common in many Southeast Asian tales, and stories promoting the Confucian hierarchy and values in many parts of East Asia.
Across the continent, however, I think you do find stories of family and its importance, stories sharing the deep values of friendship, stories of respect towards elders, among other motifs.

Since many folkloric motifs are found in many cultures, it is sometimes more important to consider how often a certain motif or theme is found in the culture.
For instance, most cultures have stories promoting cooperation and harmony.
However, in Laos, we find a much greater percentage of such stories than in most other countries. Or although all cultures have stories of war and invasion, we find a greater percentage of such tales in Korea and Vietnam, for example, because of their histories (likewise, we find a greater number of tales about resistance to invaders there).

As for common motifs in telling, I would say that across the continent, as in most of the world, you have quieter household telling styles. Then in some regions, you have a more professional, or 'outside' style, which tends to be by a man and that often has music. In East and South Asia, you find the most use of visuals in telling; the other areas don't seem to have developed that style as much.

The *Ramayana* is a classic example of a story that travelled from India to other Asian countries and was adapted seamlessly into different cultures. Are there other Asian stories that have been adapted in a similar fashion?

Although many nations and cultural groups have an epic or story that defines them (e.g. *Manas, Shahnama*), or an epic everyone knows and enjoys (*Journey to the West* – the exploits of the popular Monkey in China), these don't tend to be as widely spread as the *Ramayana* and, to a lesser extent, the *Mahabharata*. Even these two important stories are found more in South and Southeast Asia than in Central, West, or East Asia.

The Buddhist *Jakata* tales are quite popular across a large area, too, including parts of South Asia and most of Southeast Asia. The story of Vessantara (the incarnation right before the Buddha is realised) is especially popular in these areas. Likewise, the life of the Prophet and his followers, as well as some Sufi tales, are told widely over West Asia and parts of the other regions.

Today we are bombarded with stories through different media, and popular narratives – films, television, advertising – have been getting more and more homogenised under the influence of a dominant Western culture. What is the place of traditional, indigenous, culturally-specific storytelling in this context?

I'm reminded of a popular anecdote I heard. It seems that a missionary brought a television to some Native people in Canada, telling them the box knew more stories than their traditional storyteller. People eagerly flocked to the box, deserting their teller, and pleasing the missionary, who left soon after. However when he returned six months later, he found the people again gathered around the teller. The missionary, very annoyed, asked why they left the box with so many stories. Someone wisely replied, "Sir, the box does know many more stories, but our storyteller knows us!"

So I believe strongly that there will always be a place for indigenous, traditional storytelling – we just have to work harder to preserve/extend that place and role. We have to find the wonderful stories that are culture-specific and keep them alive: we can't just recycle a few old favourites that children may be bored with. We have to find those who know traditional stories and learn from them. We have to use the traditional themes and characters in new ways at times – placing them in a modern context or juxtaposing them.

Can I also add that the need for small publishers like Tulika is enormous right now. The large multinational publishers will never be committed in the same way to diverse traditional narratives and visuals.

As publishers of children's books, it is important for us to move away from dominant homogenised narratives and go towards diverse and nuanced narratives in text and visuals, as in this collection and, indeed, in all our books, so that what we offer is a rich, cultural experience. How do you feel about this?

Perhaps another small story illustrates why we do this. When I was researching the Buddhist story of Vessantara among Southeast Asian refugees in Seattle, a kind young man agreed to translate while the monk gave a telling. In the middle of the story, the man turned to me and said, "Thank you so much for bringing me here. In this fast, new world with so many things to buy, I almost forgot what is really important, but this story reminds me." *The World of Asian Stories* springs from many experiences like that, in Asia and with Asians elsewhere. We hope, through the diversity in the book, to remind readers of the incredible range of story materials across Asia – through time and place. I spent a great deal of time trying to find the voices, in story, of many Asians. I invited Asian storytellers and writers to contribute, for they know their countries best. And I tried to add poems, proverbs and riddles, true stories, journal excerpts, as well as tales of tricksters and heroes and more. From the positive feedback to Tulika's book, *The World of Indian Stories*, we felt that the addition of follow-up activities would also help readers to better explore the cultures, values, issues of today. Finally to make the book as useful as possible, we added the intros as well, to help readers get a small sense of the cultural backdrop to a story.

Some of the stories in this book may be perceived as being 'politically incorrect', as is the case with many traditional or folk stories. Another way of saying this would be that the telling borders on oversimplication. Can you explain why you chose these stories? What about all the empty spaces? And why and how does a secular, progressive person such as yourself tell such stories?

I think that a progressive person realises that the world is extremely complex and that change is a slow process. I, of course, would never include stories with blatant racist, sexist, or elitist values. But beyond that, I feel I should provide views that represent a region, as best as I can. As an outsider, no matter how much I may have studied of Asia, I don't feel competent to write the new stories of Asia for its children. I believe that that role has to be with the vibrant, talented Asian writers of today. They can look long and hard at their cultures and write the stories of change, the stories that move away from the most stereotyped ideas. If we think of the popular saying in education of giving children 'roots and wings' to grow, then I can help provide the roots and my Asian friends can give the wings.

As you explore this collection, you'll see quite a range of roles, reflecting life today and a better world, too. For instance, in the roles of women, I've included the roles of wise women ('1000 Tangas', 'The Real Work', 'The Ani and the Migoi', 'Princess Learned-in-the-Law'), courageous women ('Ly Sieng's Journey'), clever young women in traditional settings ('Give Us Rice', 'Making the Desert Bloom', 'The Patient Wife'), and the women writers who wrote 'My Father's Hands', 'Baghdad Burning', 'Growing Up', among others. You'll also find a number of stories of those who resist, trick, or challenge the powerful: 'The Flies', 'Mountain of Gems', 'Wedding Cakes'. Other tales share values – of kindness, compassion, peace, generosity ('True Worth', 'The Cows', 'The Visit', 'Paint Box', 'My Mother, Palestine').

One more thought as to story choice: I was challenged by the linguistic variety across the continent and limited to those stories translated into English. Some cultures, especially those in Central and West Asia, do not yet have a large range of stories available in English. Stories from many Asian cultures were also written down earlier by missionaries or colonial servants, who often had their own interests in mind. So it was truly a challenge to get enough good stories to choose from for this collection. Thus I freely admit that the scope of this project was too vast. It took so long to have even a beginning understanding of the continent, even though I was building on my foundation of much acquaintance with Asia. I am not sorry to have attempted this, and I thank especially Sandhya Rao and Radhika Menon for their invaluable help and vision. But I am solely responsible for the inevitable oversights and errors.

The stories in this collection seem random, even incohesive. The language, too, is minimalist. Is there a reason for this?

So many storytellers and writers helped to make this collection. Some I asked personally and I thank them profusely. Other contributions came from already published material that I found useful; I thank both writers and publishers for permissions. Since most all of these pieces were to be in the original voices of the writers (some from centuries ago), there is an inevitable random element.

However, I hoped that the reader could pull together a cohesive picture. If the writing of the tales that I retold is minimalist, that is probably the result of my concern for the readers who do not have English as a first language, and the fact that many oral folktales are rather simply told. Listeners listening to an oral story usually hear it all the way through, without a stop for tea or talk. Our memories cannot hold hundreds of words as we listen. And the tellers of folktales, by and large, are not the skilled professional tellers of epics, who can embroider and recall thousands of verses. So oral folktales by nature are easier to tell and, when written as told, are simpler to read (the spaces in such tales do, too, allow listeners to fill in the blanks and to add their own wonderful imaginations to complete the stories).

Does a story represent a culture ? How large is the scope of story per se?

I think it's rare that a story represents the totality of a culture or a people. However, great national epics like *Manas* in Kyrgystan, or the *Ramayana* in India, are said, by many people, to represent what is important and great in their cultures. Sometimes you have a character that represents an important part of the culture, too: a famous trickster like Hoja in Turkey, or a wise military hero like Admiral Yi Sun Shin of Korea.

Would you say that digital storytelling where stories are told through pictures, sound and text on the net is closer to oral than written texts and popular narratives such as film, television, advertising? Like an individual using a set of techniques to tell on the web, which also offers so much scope for personal narratives. Is it a reflection of our times where storytelling is moving from the community to the individual? How do you see oral storytelling in this context?

I love the Internet, I use it daily for communication, for sharing stories, for reaching out through my website. BUT I don't think anything can really match the exchange between oral storyteller and listener (be it one child or a village of 3000).

Oral storytelling happens in human time and human rhythms; there is human interaction. I also think that children, by their natures, need hands-on, concrete activities and often, a human being can respond to this need better than the fanciest machine. Storytelling most often happens without visuals, so that the power of the listener to imagine, to visualise, to dream is nourished as well, and not diminished by readymade images. Luckily, we don't have to choose between the two; we are very fortunate to live in a world where we can have both digital storytelling and live, oral storytelling. The two can enhance each other: spreading the art of oral storytelling and deepening the art of digital storytelling. What could be better than that?

An Introduction to Asian Tellers

Here are short profiles of some Asian tellers; there are so many other wonderful tellers to enjoy, so please keep searching.

T. S. Balakrishnan Sastrigal, one of the most accomplished of recent *harikatha* exponents in South India, spoke seven languages, knew all the major Hindu stories, was an accomplished musician and could quote about 30,000 poems and proverbs. He came to telling early in his life, but worked in a bank for quite a while as well. When he first started telling, he used to make careful scripts for his programmes. After years, he knew all the stories very well, but he still kept looking for interesting stories and anecdotes from past and present life to include in his repertoire. His programmes were usually held in the musical halls of South India, over the radio, or for various functions throughout the country. Yet he felt his favourite programmes were for the poor in Chennai, for their simplicity showed him "the real wealth of our land: the strength of our saints and the greatness of our people".

Sayakbay Karalaev is a great *manaschi*. He started to tell extracts of *Manas* in 1918, then studied under the renowned manaschi Akylbek. His variant of *Manas* consisted of 5,00,553 lines and he was skilled in improvisation. He was compared to a symphony orchestra for he changed voice and mood frequently, moving from tragic resonance to lilting melody. He sometimes cried, sometimes laughed, sometimes sighed. They say he was at times like water, at times like the desert, and all Kyrghyz people admired his talent.

Two popular Japanese tellers come from different regions and tell different tales. Lively Yokoyama Sachiko learned the stories of her home in Fukushima later in life, wanting to give to other children the story time she never gave to her children since she had to work long hours in her husband's printing business. Her style is often comic, her face very animated, her gestures strong, her timing superb. She gives popular storytelling classes to adults and performs widely in the north of Japan. She is also one of the few Japanese tellers to teach younger children to tell: guiding them in community centre classes, then helping them share their tales in a beautiful museum which was once a farmhouse.

Honda Kazu lives in elegant Kanazawa, a second Kyoto, and shares that elegance through her telling. Kazu, who came to telling some 20 years ago, performs often with musicians, wanting the audience to experience a blend of word, song and sound. Ironically, one of her earliest memories as a child is of the day she followed a *kamishibai* storyteller as a two-year old and became hopelessly lost. As her fears grew, she suddenly heard a crow caw, and found her mother, who carried her safely home. Kazu's repertoire includes older, classic poetry that she recites (e.g. *Manyoshu*), as well as the beloved tales of the modern writer Miyazawa Kenji, and newer poems like those of Tanikawa Shuntaro. Recently, she's done bilingual storytelling with American teller Cathy Spagnoli as well.

Lee Shin Ye is the future of Korean *p'ansori* singing storytelling. A very talented teen, she goes daily to Seoul's Fine Arts High School, studying school subjects in the morning, and devoting the afternoon to hours of singing. When school is done, she has private lessons with several members of a respected p'ansori family (one teacher, the youngest in that family, is trying to popularise p'ansori with the younger set by recording p'ansori in new ways more suited to ears that love rap!). During winter holidays, Shin Ye goes on a p'ansori retreat – singing loudly in the mountains as p'ansori artists trained decades ago. Shin Ye, whose voice was discovered in a middle school music class and who has already won competitions, will go on to study p'ansori in college. Her dream is to perform on the stage of Korea's National Theatre one day.

One of the best modern storytellers in Turkey was Behcet Mahir, who died in 1988. The non-literate son of a mason, he was drawn to telling after a series of important dreams, and had a large following due to his wide repertoire and his skill in oral composition. He usually told in the coffeehouses, until large video screens and other changes affected that work and he was forced to take a day job as a cleaner. His powerful voice came from a body barely five feet tall. He always told standing, so that "his 366 veins could vibrate more effectively". Mahir's telling of the *Koroglu* epic of a noble outlaw fighting oppression was legendary, going on for almost fifty hours. (Walker and Uysal: 1966, xvii–xx)

In Syria, Abu Shadi is a grocer by day but by night is a *hakawati* who tells regularly at a Damascus coffeehouse. He tries hard to build a rapport with the audience, for this is the heart of his art. "I watch them; I feel their mood," he says. "I have to be sensitive to people's problems." He tells his long epics, of Antar and other heroes, because "they tell you the right path of life. They teach virtue, they teach sacrifice, and they teach a love of the people". But the neighborhood coffeehouses have changed. Shop-owners often live away from the area now and rush home without listening, while tourists drop in but don't understand the stories. And coffeehouses themselves are closing at an alarming rate. But Abu Shadi is committed and he will continue to share his stories, as long as there are listeners to listen. (Aziz: 1996, 12-17)

The Asian storyteller still tells today to encourage devotion, to preserve heritage, to teach, to entertain and to inspire. Although some traditional forms are fading, some can be revived and spread in schools, museums and libraries, with your support. Yes, with your help and interest, in both quiet village and bustling city, Asian storytellers will tell on into the next century.

Storytelling Tools

Asian storytellers use a range of storytelling tools: words, sound effects, voice changes, gestures, silence, props, and more. This brief section introduces some ideas from various Asian styles; use the ideas as you wish in your own classroom or library.

General Advice

In several Chinese storytelling styles, certain formulas govern the techniques. Students also watch and learn from their teachers and other professional storytellers. Here are a few that give great advice for various kinds of storytelling – from telling a small true story to sharing a nightlong epic.

Say what should be said,
Don't say what shouldn't be said.

Sing not just with the voice,
But with the heart.

Learn hard and practice hard.

While on the stage, perform.
While off the stage, observe.

In Iran, Mulla Husayn-i Kashifi summarised eight rules of storytelling:

First if one is a beginner, the storyteller must have studied the tale that one wants to tell with a master; and if one is experienced, one must have practised it beforehand, so that one may not get stuck in telling it.

Second one must begin with eloquence, speak in an exciting manner, and not be plain or boring in one's discourse.

Third one must know what kind of narration is fitting for what kind of assembly, and how much to simplify, and so on. The storyteller should narrate more of what one's audience likes.

Fourth one should occasionally embellish the prose with verse. However, one should be careful not to bore people with it; as the great ones have said, "Verse in storytelling is like salt in food; if it is not enough, the food will be bland, and if it is too much, the dish will be salty."

Fifth one should not utter impossible statements, nor should one hyperbolise lest one should appear silly to his audience.

Sixth one should not make sarcastic or critical remarks lest one become an object of dislike.

Seventh one should not demand payment forcefully, nor should one pester the audience for it.

Eighth one must neither stop too soon, nor go on too late; but must always keep to the path of moderation. (Omidsalar, 1999: 335)

Repertoire, Recall, and Form

In many Asian traditions, the story repertoire was passed down from master to disciple or parent to child. One learned the same stories one heard. Modern Asian tellers have a wider range of material to choose from, and many books and CDs/tapes to help them. They consider a story's appeal to teller and audience, the complexity of the tale, the elements of drama, the range of language, the possibilities for gesture or music, and so on.

To remember the story, an epic teller will often use many formulas and set phrases/descriptions to embroider a skeletal plot. Other professional tellers often learn the story from a master, bit by bit: listening then repeating. A traditional teller of folktales will hear a tale several times then repeat it in her own words, embellishing it with style perhaps, but not changing the basic form. Various tellers across Asia might agree with this popular Chinese formula:

> *To memorise the master's words a thousand times is not as effective as seeing the master in actual performance. And to see the master's performance a thousand times is not as effective as performing it yourself.*

Modern Asian tellers often use visualisation and repetition to learn older tales, sometimes mapping the story or making a brief outline. When creating new stories or shaping true tales, they experiment with form: beginning with a hook/opening, building up the story at the right pace, weaving in humour or suspense, then ending with a satisfying conclusion, at the right time!

Sound

The Voice

Many Asian tellers use their voices in expressive ways, for the voice is a basic tool in telling. Perhaps the voice with the greatest range is that of the p'ansori teller from Korea who once trained by shouting near waterfalls. Chinese tellers of old had voices that made the walls of the teahouse rattle when they did a fighting scene, while some Malay tellers today use a chant-like tone, without great differences of pitch or volume, but still compelling.

Another interesting voice effect comes from speed: saying a list of words, or rhythms, at a very fast speed, as the p'ansori teller does at times. And of course, there is the absence of voice – silence/a pause. This can be a very effective tool, when used as Chinese teller Wu Tianxu did 200 years ago:

When he came to the point where Zhang Fei's voice makes the bridge fall down, he first put up a face like he was going to shout...but he would only open his mouth, roll his eyes and gesture with his hands, but still no sound. Even so, in the hall packed with listeners, everyone had the impression of an earthshaking thunder striking their ears. He commented: '...To equal the voice of Zhang Fei, instead of making the sound with my mouth, I made it spring from everybody's heart'. (Bordahl: 2002, 63).

Sound Effects

Some Asian traditions make wonderful use of sound effects. The Japanese language probably has the greatest range of sound words, see just a few below, but all languages have some to share (and new ones can be created as well).

no-shi, no-shi	(noe-shee)	heavy walk of elephant
kappo kappo	(kahp-poe)	sound of horse's hoofs
doshin	(doe - shin)	something heavy falling
gacha gacha	(gah - chah)	rattle, clatter
niko niko	(nee - koe)	to smile warmly
pacha pacha	(pah - chah)	a light splash
wan wan	(wahn)	dog's bark

This passage from a p'ansori story shows a haunting and effective use of sound words:

> The wind sweeps '*Urururururr!*'
> As if the earth were wreathing and writhing.
> A hard rain pours.
> The night bird calls, '*Puuk! Puuk!*'
> Water drip-drops, '*Cchrurururururu!*'
> Elf-fliers flash, '*Hweeii! Hweeii!*'
> The ghosts whisper,
> '*Turun turun turun turun!*'
> By twos, by threes, they stir and weep,
> *Iiiii─────!*
> *Iiiii──Iiiiii─────*
> *iii─────!*
> (Park: 2003, 201)

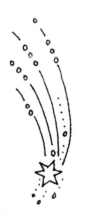

Language

No matter which of the many Asian languages tellers use, they use it well, often with rich descriptions and an ear for the sound of words. Repetition – of a sound, a word, a phrase – is another tool often used, very common in longer epics, where formulas are also inserted to help the memory. Consider these examples:

From West Asia come two common means of transport:

> *The camel*   running like a flock of ostriches or a fallen star

pads round and smooth like newly minted coins
with copper nose rings sparkling in the sun
tails like stalks of date bunches with little fruit

The car O driver of a car that struts on the road as a champion...and
streaks along like a falcon...to swoop down on a flock of
bustards it spotted in the desert's vastness.

I pray to God to preserve it from the evil eye of the envious when it
roars full throttle over the glistening, flint-strewn plains...carrying lion-
like passengers. (Kurpershoek: 1994, 269)

From China comes a linked image of a far temple:

Hills growing dark clouds
Clouds covering green pines
Pines hiding the old temple
The temple sheltering a hillside monk
The hillside monk in Buddha's hall strikes the wooden fish
(Stevens: 1972, 239)

From Malaysia, a list describing a hero:

Sitting down, he counts his many beauty spots.
Beauty spots on the flanks, a bat's elbow,
Beauty spots on his breast, a turtledove's footprints,
Beauty spots on the arms, marching ants,
Beauty spots on the back, a shower of rain,
Beauty spots on the neck, fighting quails,
Beauty spots on the calf, traps for fish,
Beauty spots on the chin, bumblebees taking shelter...
(Derks: 1994, 637)

Beginnings and Endings

Rituals, offerings, invocations, and prayers start and end many storytelling
events in Asia. In Malaysia, a programme by the *awang batil* Malay teller
begins with *makan pinang,* introduction, where the storyteller chews betel
leaves, and burns incense to purify the area around him; they say that if the
incense is not burnt, the storyteller will forget his stories. Then he is given
tobacco, betel leaves, incense, jugs of ice-cold water and tamarind juice,
along with a monetary gift. After that, he invokes blessings to protect the
performance and begins the story.

In more informal settings, inside the home, short formulas to start and
end the tale may still be used.

Some Beginnings

"*Bismillah al-Rahman al-Rahim*" (In the name of God, the Merciful, the
Compassionate: in some Islamic countries)

"In olden times, in times when rams were still without horns and sheep without tails, there lived..." (Kazakhstan)

"Once in Korea when tigers smoked long pipes ..." (Korea)

"*Mukashi, mukashi*" (mu kah shee) Long, long ago.... (Japan)

"*Dangbo, dingbo*" Long ago.... (Bhutan)

And Endings

"They have had their wish fulfilled;
Let's go up to their bedstead." (Turkey)

"Garland of gold to the listener,
garland of flowers to the teller.
May this tale go to heaven
and come down to be told again." (Nepal)

At times, the teller, pestered by demands for more stories, uses a tiny 'endless' tale like this one, made up by a Korean grandfather, to tire his listeners:

> Once a farmer went to dig in his field. On a hill, he found a metal watermelon and wanted to send it home. So he pushed the round melon down the hill and it rolled and rolled and rolled...(The children asked, "Then what happened?")
> "It rolled and rolled and rolled."
> ("Then what?") "It rolled and rolled and rolled."
> ("And then..?") It's still rolling and rolling and...."

Gesture

Some Asian tellers use generous gestures, while others, like many Japanese library storytellers, believe that the story should be shared almost completely through the words spoken. The position and stance of the teller, too, varies from setting to setting, style to style. Here are a few examples.

The Japanese *rakugo* teller kneels on a cushion and shows different characters by shifting his face and chest and, at times, by lifting himself up slightly on his knees.

The manaschi, telling the *Manas* epic in Kyrgyzstan, may use wide, dramatic arm motions and an animated face, either sitting or standing.

The harikatha teller of South India usually sits cross-legged, using arms, eloquent hand gestures, and facial expressions, or tells from a standing position, using the whole body and even pacing at times.

The Chinese *ping-tan tanci* storyteller, who often plays a stringed instrument, sits upright, holding the instrument on her lap, next to a table that also holds tea. When not playing, the teller puts down the instrument and may stand and use some hand gestures as she narrates.

The *ottan thullal* storyteller of Kerala, India, uses his whole body: swaying, posing, doing small dance steps, and making eloquent hand gestures known as mudras.

Humour

Humour is a welcome tool of the teller; it can be used in a wide range of stories: to provide relief, to poke fun, to warm up the audience, to exaggerate, to surprise, and more. An Iranian teller described how the hero killed a witch in this way, "The hero stepped forth, and without asking permission, beheaded the witch Sahana, and Sahana duly died, because in those days it was often the case that those who were beheaded, also died."

He went on to tell of a strong woman who seized a man and "swung him around her head and so skillfully smashed him upon the ground that he was not hurt at all, except for the fact that no part of his body was left unharmed. Indeed, there was nothing wrong with him apart from the fact that he expired on the spot". (Omidsalar: 1999, 337)

Improvisation and Collaboration

Improvisation is used in some Asian storytelling forms. In many Central Asian epic traditions, improvisation allowed the teller to adapt to different audiences: praising the family heritage of rich listeners or mocking the rich when telling to the poor! Indian tellers in some styles use improvisation to keep the old epics relevant for today's listeners: weaving in side stories, jokes, comments, news stories and proverbs.

In the *chakyar koothu* style of South India, the teller could improvise insults and warnings to the king himself. Joseph Kunnath, a story lover from Kerala, told me of a Chakyar who wished to remind the king that his ministers were rather dull-witted. Thus he told of Hanuman as a huge monkey, jumping from rock to rock. When he said, "And Hanuman jumped from empty spot to empty spot to empty spot", the teller pointed to each of the ministers' heads, one after another after another. And from my journal comes a recent example:

> As my husband, Sivam, and I sat eagerly listening to the Chakyar describe Sita's long-ago marriage, the Chakyar suddenly noticed me, the only pale face in a sea of sandalwood colour. Pointing my way, he said, "Sita's marriage was so grand that white faces came from far away to attend, even though they didn't understand anything."
>
> Everyone laughed, I blushed, and just then Sivam decided to take a photo of the audience. As he walked up front to shoot, the teller's expressive eyes slowly followed him in absolute silence. Right after the camera's bright flash, the teller's hand swept dramatically toward Sivam and he cried, "Even big-shot photographers came from New York City to steal photographs of Sita and Rama." The crowd loved it!

Props

Many Asian storytellers have long used props, from fans and scrolls to unfolding story boxes. Visual storytelling props appear to be most popular in South and East Asia. In West Asia, the major form with visuals is the *pardehdari* in Iran, while in Central Asia, the epics were told often with music, but not visuals. Southeast Asia boasts several fine puppetry traditions, but few visual props, although the awang batil storyteller in northern Malaysia uses brightly covered masks at times for his characters, and some Malay tellers like to twist and fold a handkerchief into the objects in a story.

In East Asia, temple scrolls were used earlier in Japan, while kamishibai (picture cards) flourished in Japan in the last century and continue today. A *thangka* scroll painting was used by some to tell the great epic, *King Gesar*, in Tibet, and folding fans are used for dramatic effect in Korean p'ansori, while both a fan and a hand towel are used to represent objects in Japanese rakugo. Yet it is in South Asia that one still finds the richest range of visual props, from the large *phad* (horizontal scroll) and *kavad* (story box) to the older *chitra katha* cards and the *pata* (vertical scroll), all from India. And in Bangladesh, some tellers use long scarves – as a rope, whip, horse's reins, turban, baby, or sari.

Music

Music is very much a part of many Asian storytelling styles. Instruments are often stringed (the Japanese *biwa*, Sumatran *rabab*, the Chinese *p'i p'a*) or percussive: the *mridangam* of the Indian harikatha teller, the bamboo clappers of the Chinese clapper tales, the brass bowl of some Malay tellers, even the cane used by the Syrian hakawati teller. At times, the instrument accompanies a song, at other times it is merely melodic. Some ballad story forms are told entirely in song. Most styles require much practice and training, but some tellers use only simple rhythms and drumbeats to add interest and mood.

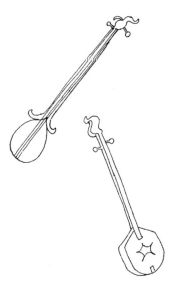

Audience Participation and Response

Storytellers in Asian libraries in Singapore, Japan, and some other countries might encourage audience participation – especially from young audiences – in the form of a song, chant, or gesture that the audience does with the teller. This type of participation is rarely found in most Asian folk and professional traditions. But listeners of varied ages might respond simply with a head movement, or a word – the *chota* (nice), *olsigu* (excellent), *kurochi* (perfect) of the p'ansori audience in Korea – to show their enjoyment.

The Arab storyteller, too, depends upon audience response as listeners make criticisms and objections at times. Yet the minangkabau tellers, seen by Nigel Philips in West Sumatra, Indonesia, seemed to make little effort to relate to the audience, gazing into the distance or singing with their eyes closed. (Phillipps: 1981, 67)

Many modern Asian tellers, though, in front of a demanding audience today use the power of eye contact. They 'read' the audience to know if the story is reaching or not, and they note any signs of distraction. This sensitivity is especially needed now since many audiences, raised on computers and televisions, often find it hard to concentrate on a story told simply.

Another problem arises from content, as many traditional Asian tellers have a hard time using yesterday's material with the young people of today. Thus, not only sensitivity is needed, but also the flexibility to adapt old material to new needs, or to find different material altogether. Without a means of change, certain styles will be lost.

Romli Mahmud, perhaps the last awang batil teller in Malaysia at this point, feels that the audience now finds the old stories boring and longwinded. He sadly says, "The art cannot survive; life has changed. It is just a matter of time before my instruments and masks are taken over by the museum." (Koswanage: 2002, 1)

Putting It All Together

Now that you have a few more ideas from the amazing world of Asian storytelling, use them to help keep the art form alive and growing. Pick and choose ideas from this chapter, and add them to telling tips you've gathered elsewhere. Remember, too, that the setting can help you – Asian tellers share stories in a range of places, from nomadic tents and temples to village centres, homes, libraries, schools, and more. When you're ready to tell, make the storytelling setting as comfortable as can be. Keep noise to a minimum and lights dimmed; have listeners sit on the floor/ground in front of you if possible, use a microphone only if essential.

As you continue telling, remember that varied tellers have varied strengths, so find and use your own talents. Remember, too, that different stories may need different techniques – some work better with more sounds, some with a quiet voice, some with more action or music, etc. Use your judgement, which will grow as you keep telling. Choose the stories you like and tell with warmth and sensitivity to your audience. Nourish your storytelling skills: try to find tellers to watch, read more about the art form, expand your repertoire. Deepen your research into Asian cultures so that you avoid cultural mistakes, enrich the story materials here, and add bits of Asian languages, too. Help your students by storytelling follow-up activities. And when you try the activities, improvise if needed: adapt directions and supplies for the ages of your students and for your local resources.

Stories do indeed weave magic around our globe. Through our stories, we try on roles, dream, learn about ourselves, and touch others. As we look across the rich and varied Asian cultures through stories, we appreciate how we differ and recognise what we share. Storytelling helps us to travel the world. Enjoy your journey...

Stories and Activities
Central Asia

Russian Federation

ASTANA

Kazakhstan

Aral
Sea

Caspian Sea

Uzbekistan

Turkmenistan

ASHKABAD

TASHKENT

BISHKEK

Kyrgyzstan

Iran

China

DUSHANBE

Tajikistan

Afghanistan

THE REGION

THE WIDE, OPEN SPACES OF CENTRAL ASIA have drawn traders, saints, conquerors, and others over the centuries. Across its varied lands trekked merchants on the famed Silk Route, who brought silk, spices, and stories on their travels East and West. Although the area boasts of almost every geographical feature known – from deserts to mountain peaks, from rich valleys to wild rivers – it is the Steppes that helped to define and determine the unique culture and character of the region. The Steppes have many moods and dresses: dusty or ice-covered, empty or full of spring blooms; and throughout the seasons, they demand contemplation and reward courage.

Through Central Asia, in its earliest centuries, roamed nomads who followed their herds. A more settled group also emerged, creating the early cities, which were Persian; yet later Turkic culture established itself as well. In the fourth century BCE, Alexander of Macedonia conquered the region briefly. After some more time, the trade of the Silk Route began and flourished. In these pre-Islamic times, the dominant religion was Zoroastrianism. However, in the seventh century, the forces of Islam arrived and with the famous battle of Talas in 750 CE between the Chinese and the Muslim armies, Islam was finally dominant.

In the eighth and ninth centuries, Muslim art and culture flourished in a grand manner. Bukhara, with its heritage of Persian art, was the cultural centre of Central Asia in the ninth and tenth centuries, attracting scholars from across the Muslim world. However, the Mongols on their steeds proved an invincible force over the next period of Central Asian history and by 1206, Genghis Khan ruled over one of the largest empires in the world, covering Central Asia and beyond. The Mongols used great force and violence, at times, but also made the region more safe and orderly. Mongol women were a strong force, taught to defend the empire and not forced to marry.

With so much of the region under strict Mongol control, trade, cultural exchange, and other economic activity flourished. The old city of Samarkand became the new capital of the powerful ruler Timur (Tamarlane in the West) in the late fourteenth century. He began vast building projects that still inspire – the turquoise domes of mosques and tombs, and the awe-inspiring Registan Square – and that gave the city names like 'Jewel of Islam' or 'Garden of the Soul'. Yet that empire, too, fell to fights and internal problems. Then, from 1853 to 1873, the Russian Empire moved in from the north through a series of military conquests. Settlers followed and by 1865, Russia controlled much of the region. Changes came as many farmers were forced to grow cotton on a large scale, and nomads found their traditional roaming lifestyle blocked by new construction.

The Russian Revolution ended the rule of the Russian Empire and, although a revolutionary spirit took seed, Central Asian efforts towards independence were crushed by the Soviets. In 1917, another blow came when a famine in the region brought ruin as well. Soon after that, the Basmachi Turkistan liberation movement began, using as its inspiration the epic, *Koroglu,* about the sixteenth century hero who fought for freedom against all odds. However, by 1931, the resistance ended.

During this time, the republics of Central Asia were carved out of the region and, although they were to reflect ethnic identities, the borders often created more divisions and problems. By the early 1950s, things settled somewhat and a period of stability continued for some thirty years. Then, dramatic changes began in the Soviet Union, and when it finally dissolved in 1991, the five republics became independent nations.

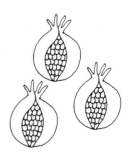

It has not been an easy task, though, to establish strong economies and to provide opportunity for all. Many members of the ruling class, including scientists and teachers, returned to Russia. Corruption is an issue for most of these countries and the ecological damage from Soviet rule remains a daunting challenge. One major problem arose when huge canals diverted water from the Aral Sea, to irrigate large tracts of land for cotton and wheat. The Aral Sea started to shrink, noticeably by the 1970s. Former port cities became landlocked while loose sands and chemicals from heavy pesticides/fertilisers filled the air, creating severe health risks for the region.

The role of women has traditionally been a freer one in Central Asia: in nomad families, the women often had to care for the entire household for part of the year if men needed to fight or hunt. Later, under the Russians, those Islamic women who were veiled were forced to give them up. Many women were educated – literacy rates remain high throughout the region – and urged to be part of the work force. Today, women here, as elsewhere, face challenges as they juggle the tasks of motherhood and outside work. Yet both women and men share the many stories of this vital region: tales of heroes, saints, tricksters, and more.

. . . and its STORIES

Across Central Asia, the oral epics were great favourites. Every area had its heroes, shared through the memory and voice of the teller. The most famous is *Manas*, the national epic of Kyrgyzstan that tells of the great hero, Manas, his 40 knights, his son, and grandson. Manaschi tellers who specialised in this story needed days, even weeks, to perform this using more than 20 varieties of melodies, gestures and mimicry. But shorter pieces were spread by others who knew some of the fine poetry. The parts with stories and descriptions were spoken at a faster speed while the dialogue and speeches were shared more solemnly. One of the world's longest epics – some versions have over 5,00,000 lines – it shares rich cultural details of feasts, games, armour, weddings and daily life, while it also inspires and unites the Kyrgyz people to this day.

In Turkmenistan, the *dastan* (epics) are told by *bakhshi*, who may play a two-stringed instrument as they share narratives, often the beloved epic of *Koroglu*, the hero of Turkmen resistance. There are indeed many Turkic epics that share and shape ethnic identity and cultural values. Most commemorate liberation struggles and are about the *alp* (hero) who fights against invaders or traitors from among his own people.

Among the nomadic peoples of Central Asia, many poet-bards are thought to be close to the spirits, to the world of the shaman. The Uzbek word 'bakhshi' can be used for bards or shamans, and both can be called to their work initially by a dream or an unusual experience.

These long epics were often put together, as in many oral epic styles, from formulas and set descriptions. Such elements might include the birth and childhood of a hero, details about armour, weapons and battle, glories of strong horses, the beauty of the hero's bride, and so on. Also popular to this day in much of Central Asia is the verbal dual between bards or poets. Known for its complex language and fast-paced wit, the contests attract a range of listeners eager to enjoy the linguistic virtuosity displayed.

Kazakhstan

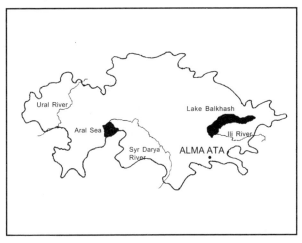

Antelope, sand cat and jerboa roam in the desert and semi-arid landscape of Kazakhstan, which is surrounded by the Caspian Sea, the Altai mountains, the plains of West Siberia, and the deserts of Central Asia. Kazakhstan, the world's ninth largest country, is famous for its Steppes, the world's largest grassland, and the rivers Ili, Irtysh, Ishim and Ural that cross it. The official state language of this fossil fuel and mineral rich nation is Kazakh, but Russian is recognised as a national language and Russians still number about 30 per cent of the population. While some Kazakhs follow Islam, there are some who practice the traditional Tengriism. Carpet-weaving is a practical Kazakh craft, with the ram's horn being the most popular motif. But one of the most admired arts is that of the *akyn* storytellers of Kazakhstan and Kyrgyzstan who duel through improvised poems in contests (*Aytis*) while playing the *dombra* stringed instrument. Family storytellers too pass on tales, like this clever one collected by Sally Pomme Clayton.

A Whole Brain

IT WAS THE SEVENTH DAY. God had finished making the world and at last he could rest — when he realised he had forgotten something. He had forgotten to give human beings brains. So he took a jug, filled it with brains, called the Angel Gabriel and said, "Go and give human beings brains!"

Gabriel flew down to Earth and saw people everywhere. There were so many people but there was only one jug. There were not enough brains to go round. So Gabriel gave each person a drop. Then he flew back to heaven with the empty jug.

When God looked down on creation, he saw that people were very unhappy. They were arguing and fighting. There was hunger, poverty and tears. People did not understand how to live together at all.

"Oh dear," said God, "human beings have only got a quarter of a brain each. I'd better make someone with a whole brain who can sort them all out."

So God made one more person and filled that brain right up to the top. He filled the brain with stories, songs, poems and sparkling words. And he sent the storyteller down to Earth to tell stories and sing songs, to tell and sing wisdom back into foolish human beings.

It is there where you put it down. When you take it in your hands, it speaks.

A book.

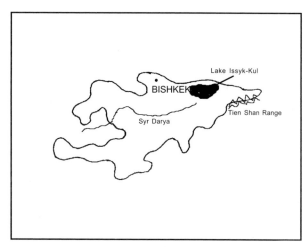

Kyrgyzstan

Kyrgyzstan is a land of mountains and beauty; its name means 'land of 40 tribes'. Turks, Mongols, Uzbeks, Russians all settled in this region before it became an independent country in 1991. Known as the Switzerland of Central Asia, it is dominated by the Tien Shan mountains with the Kakshaal-Too range bordering China. Lake Issyk-kul is the second biggest mountain lake in the world and Kyrgyzstan has the world's largest natural walnut forest. While the Kyrgyz are the most populous ethnic group in the region, Russians, Uzbeks, Tatars, Uyghurs, Kazakhs and Ukrainians also live there. Women weave beautiful textiles from the felt of sheep and all people are inspired by *Manas*, the long, traditional epic poem of the Kyrgyz people that is highly regarded as an oral composition and a national treasure. The short tale below is not part of that long epic, but is a very interesting tale with a strong message, shared in the present tense by Prof. Ilse Cirtautas in Seattle.

The Hawk and the Owl

So many countries,
so many traditions.
– a Kyrgyz saying

ONE DAY A HAWK meets a sick owl living in a place where she cannot find any food. Unselfishly, the hawk takes care of the owl, better even than of himself. In the end, the two embrace each other and become friends. Together they fly to a far-off place. Because of the hawk's hunting skills, they have a good life. The owl completely recovers and soon is able to find her own food.

One day, while flying out to hunt, the owl says, "From now on each of us should live separately." Searching here and there and everywhere, they are not able to find any food.

Thereupon the owl, calling the hawk to come close to her, quickly seizes the hawk and says, "I will eat you." The hawk weeps and reminds the owl of their eternal friendship and how much he has helped her.

But the owl responds, "To return kindness for kindness is the sign of a donkey; to return evil for kindness is the mark of a saintly person. To live in this world means to rob, to fight and, if this is not enough, to suppress, to deceive and to do everything for one's own good living."

Saying this, the owl presses so hard on the hawk that he shrieks out in pain. With her sharp claws resembling iron forks, the owl kills the hawk and after devouring him, she flaps her wings and flies away.

talk about
What's fair, what's not.
Is justice always just?

Tajikistan

Tajikistan is said to come from Tajik, the crown or *taj* of the Pamir Knot (the junction of three mountain ranges). The Persians, the Sassanids, the Greeks, the Arabs, the Russians – all left an indelible mark on the country which became independent in 1991 but was then plunged into civil war until 1997. Mainly mountainous, with the Trans-Alay in the north and the Pamirs in the southeast, Tajikistan's main rivers are the Amu Darya and the Panj; their basins are the Fergana, the Kafirnigan, and the Vaksh valleys where wildflowers abound. Up in the mountains the Marco Polo sheep, the yak and the snow leopard make their home. Tajikistan, the smallest Central Asian country, is renowned for its weaving and printing traditions, and *zardosi* embroidery. The Persian influence in arts, the glories of Tajik cities on the Silk Road, and the courage of leaders like Zarina, below, give the country a proud heritage.

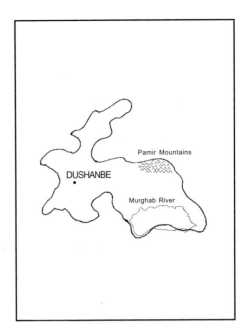

Making the Desert Bloom

ONCE, AMONG THE BRAVE TAJIKS, there lived a *padishah* with 40 strong sons. One day, they went to hunt hawks then, several days later, started home with their catch. But all of a sudden they stopped. For in the distance, they saw a line of 40 young women come gracefully down a steep mountain trail. Each one carried a pot upon her head and stepped like a fine gazelle. They went to a river there, filled their pots, then walked back up and over the mountain.

"Go now," said the padishah to his minister. "Send messengers to follow them and find out if they are *peris* or real women!" As the messengers galloped off, the padishah and his sons turned again toward home. When they were still a day's journey away, the messengers returned.

"Sir," one said with respect, "they are indeed human. They are the 40 daughters of a great padishah who lives in a kingdom with no water. So every day, his daughters spend hours to fetch precious water. He has offered his lovely daughters in marriage to any who can make a passage through the mountain, to bring water into his land."

Overjoyed, the padishah and his sons sent rich gifts with offers of marriage. Then they called for many workers to help dig through the mountain. For 40 long days and nights, workers dug until at last a beautiful stream of blue reached the parched land. There was a grand celebration and everyone rejoiced as the 40 couples were then married.

The youngest daughter, Zarina, married the youngest son, Bahodur, and they made the most handsome couple of all. Both shared warm hearts and spirits that loved nature. Zarina spent hours walking on the banks of the precious new river, planting seeds, and helping the birds and small animals that also loved her kind heart.

At last it was time for the sons to return home with their new wives. But as they all rode on, suddenly there appeared a large whirlwind of sand, right in their

Bite a big piece of bread, but don't speak much.
– *a Tajik saying*

way. It moved to the right and to the left, blocking their path in all directions. Bahodur soon went up to see what it was.

"AHHHHH!" came a fierce cry, for it was a *dev*, a monster, in the midst of the sand. "You are so small, you little Bahodur! I've come to stop you, for you cannot take away that Zarina, who ruined my desert with her plants. Give her to me and then you can live."

"Never!" cried Bahodur. "She will never go with you!"

"Then I'll destroy your fine new channel and bury both of your kingdoms under the sand!" roared the dev. Zarina, who heard the terrible words, now rode up to Bahodur.

"I must go," she said, "or he will destroy us all." The others pleaded with her, they offered to fight, although they knew that the dev had powerful magic. But Zarina insisted, so at last she left with Bahodur, who refused to leave her. Bravely the two galloped up to the dev and soon vanished in the swirling sands as the dev carried them off to a dark underground cave.

"Sleep now," he said, "for tomorrow you will die!" Then he turned and started to snore, blocking the entrance. As the two looked fearfully around, Zarina suddenly saw a box on a stone, and remembered her grandmother's words. "Look," she said eagerly, "they say that inside the box is another box and inside that is the soul of the dev, in a bird. If we can kill that bird, the dev will die."

The stones of my river
are as soft as a pillow.
– a Tajik saying

Now strong with new hope, Bahodur crept to the box and pulled at the large sword hanging nearby. Freeing it, he hit the box with all his strength. At once it broke, but it woke the dev as well.

With a horrid roar, the dev reached for Bahodur, who quickly thrust his sword through the second box and into the bird's heart.

"AHHHHHHHHHH!" The dev sank to the earth with a huge cry of rage, then was silent. Overjoyed, the young couple climbed out of the cave and started across the desert. Fortune smiled, for they managed to capture two wild horses.

Imagine the faces of those lost in pain when they saw the two coming back from the dead. There was great feasting and dancing as everyone welcomed them. Yet, just then, in the midst of joy, a messenger came with terrible news.

"Hurry," he called, "you must all return. Our enemies have taken the city and wait for you outside the gates, to capture and kill you all." At once the men put on their battle gear and raced across the Steppes to meet the challenge. As the brave brothers swooped down to fight the enemy, the wives watched anxiously. But although the padishah, his sons, and servants fought like lions, the enemy was too strong. It seemed that all was lost, that all would die. But then brave Zarina called to her sisters, "Tie your clothes and hair and prepare to do battle."

Soon, looking like men, the women raced down with great cries as Zarina pounded her tambourine. Hearing such terrible sounds and seeing such fierce-looking soldiers, the enemy thought that a large army had come. They grew confused and lost their spirit. Some were easily killed, others turned to run, others gave up in defeat.

At last, in great spirits once again, the victors entered the city in peace. There they all dwelt happily, and often told the tale of brave Zarina and Bahodur, who made the desert bloom, killed the dev and saved two kingdoms.

Turkmenistan

The Persian Achaemenids, the Greeks to the Arabs and Turks to the Russians – they all invaded and occupied the region that finally became independent Turkmenistan in 1991. Today, Turkmenistan has Central Asia's most homogeneous population, along with the world's fifth largest natural gas reserves. Home to the Karakum desert, it is bound by the Caspian Sea, the Balkan mountains and the Kugitang range. Although the official language is Turkmen, the various tribes often communicate through Russian, and are known for their exquisite embroidery and weaving. Their colourful *gilliam* rugs, different for different clans, are world famous. Travelling musicians, called bakhshi, can still be heard across the land singing to the accompaniment of the *dutar*. Many stories are told as well, including those of the popular, clever character, Mirali.

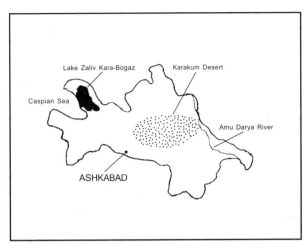

The Mountain of Gems

ONCE IN THE LAND now called Turkmenistan, there lived a poor widow and her son, Mirali. The two worked hard and lived very simply, but every day was a struggle. Finally, one day the mother said, "My dear son, there is no one to hire you here. You must leave now and find some work quickly to help us survive."

Grass grows from its own roots.
– *a Turkmen saying*

So the next day, he set off, promising to return as soon as possible. On and on he walked but he could find no work at all. He grew worried and sad until he suddenly saw the home of a rich *bai* in the distance. He went up and bowed to him, then asked politely if there was work to be done.

"You look strong and honest," said the bai. "I'll give you some work. Rest tonight to prepare."

Happily, Mirali spread his blanket and soon slept, to be ready for his new job. But the next day, although he was fed well, there was no work for him. The next day, too, passed with good food but no work, and the next. At last, Mirali went again to the bai and said, "When will I start working, sir?"

"We leave tomorrow," replied the bai. "And to prepare for our journey, please kill one of the cows, skin it, then pack the skin." Mirali did as instructed, then soon evening fell and he moved into the land of dreams.

In the cold morning, the two started off on horseback. After hours of riding, they stopped at the base of a tall, steep cliff.

"Put the cowhide on the ground, with the hair facing up," said the bai, and Mirali did. "Now lie down on the skin." Very perplexed, Mirali followed instructions. At once, the bai tied the skin around Mirali. Just then, two huge birds flew down and picked up the skin, with Mirali inside. As he cried out, the birds flew to the top of the cliff and put him down. But he struggled so much to get out that he scared them away. When he was free, he looked down at the bai.

"Why am I here? Get me down," he cried.

"Wait," the rich man replied. "First you have to get some gems for us. Look around and you'll see the jewels. Throw them down to me."

Surely enough, all around him were shining reds, greens and whites. Quickly, Mirali threw some gems down, then said, "Now help me down."

"Throw a few more and I'll tell you how to get down," promised the rich man. Mirali threw more and more until the bai cried, "That's enough."

"Now tell me how to come down," called Mirali.

"Just find my other servants who are there, and ask them," laughed the bai. "Perhaps they can help." Then he rode happily away with his bags of jewels.

Mirali walked slowly around and suddenly saw hundreds of bones scattered on the ground. He stared in horror as he tried desperately to think of a plan. All of a sudden, he heard the sound of giant wings and a huge bird swooped down. Quickly, Mirali grabbed hold of its legs and when the bird flew off, Mirali did too. As the bird flew near the earth, Mirali let go and fell down into a tree. Brushing himself off with a great sigh, he went back to the town. He cut his hair and changed his clothes, then went back to the bai, asking for work.

Of course, the greedy rich man didn't recognise him and so hired him at once. Several days later, the two set off again to the mountain. But this time, when the skin was on the ground and the bai told the servant to lie down, Mirali said, "I'm sorry, sir, but can you show me exactly how to do it?" Shaking his head, the bai lay down, and at once Mirali tied him up. The birds came just then and picked up the screaming bai. When they left him on the top of the mountain he looked down and suddenly recognised Mirali.

"How did you get down?" he cried.

"First throw me some jewels," called Mirali, "and then I'll tell you." So the rich man threw down piles and piles of gems until his arms ached. Mirali packed up all the gems, then got on the horse.

"Now tell me the secret," cried the bai. "Where is the path down?"

"Ah, you'll have to ask your servants up there," cried Mirali as he turned to go. "Perhaps they can help you." And as that cruel and greedy man kept shouting into the wind, Mirali rode back to his mother. And the two lived in peace, without worry, for the rest of their days.

The fish rots from the head.
– a Turkmen saying

talk about
Speaking up for oneself. Why do we sometimes want to take revenge?

Uzbekistan

The region now known as Uzbekistan was inhabited by the Persians, the Greeks, the Parthians, the Sassanids, the Russians and was, until it became independent in 1991, a part of the USSR. Now the country is largely populated by Russians, Tajiks, Kazakhs and others, although the Uzbeks are in the majority. A fifth of the land is occupied by the Turan Lowlands. It also has the Tien Shan and Pamir mountains, the Qizilqun desert, and the rivers Amu Darya and Syr Darya. The rare Saiga antelope and the desert monitor lizard are found in Uzbekistan. *Shash mugam*, a form of classical Islamic court music, is still widely popular,

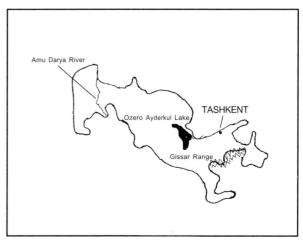

as also ceramics, miniature toy-making, calligraphy and miniature painting. A range of rich cultural traditions were passed on in cities famed along the Silk Route here, like Samarkand and Tashkent, the setting for the next story.

1000 Tangas

LONG AGO, A MAN came from a far village to work in lovely Tashkent. He did the lowliest of jobs, sweeping and wiping and cleaning for others. And every time he received two coins for his labour, he used one to buy a little bread and saved one to take home. In this way, after many years, he had saved up the very fine sum of 1000 *tangas*.

"Soon," he thought, "I will have enough to go back to my village and live happily. But since I have such a good sum now, I must be careful. It might be stolen from me if I keep it in my poor room." So he decided to leave it with the *kashi*, the judge, who was said to be honest and wise.

He went before the man, bowed and asked him to watch the bag of coins for some time.

"I shall guard this as if it was my own treasure, you need not fear," said the kashi. The villager left, content. Soon, a year had passed, and he was at last ready to return home. He went to the kashi, asking for his bag.

"What bag, you beggar?" cried the kashi. "Why would I have any of your money here? I have my own. Be gone before my guards throw you out."

Not believing his ears, the poor man stumbled out. He wandered the streets crying and shaking his head. Finally, a kind woman came up to him and asked what was wrong. When the man told his sad tale, the woman smiled slowly and said, "Come home, I think I can help you."

At her fine house, she gave him dates and cool water. Then she called her son and showed him a large box.

"Dear boy," she said. "This man and I are going to the kashi. You must follow without anyone seeing. Hide and watch what we do. When you see the kashi reach out his hands to take this box, run into the room and cry, 'Mother, father just returned with his camels and goods.'"

Measure cloth seven times.
Cut once just right.
– *an Uzbek saying*

31

After the boy agreed, the woman told the man what he should do. Finally, satisfied with the arrangements, she dressed in her richest clothes and went to the kashi, carrying the box gracefully on her head. She was welcomed warmly into his home.

"How can I help you, dear lady?" asked the kashi, seeing her fine, expensive clothes.

"Excuse me, but since my husband, the merchant Rahim, is away, I fear for our treasure with no one to guard it. So I have placed all of our gold and jewels in this box and I wish to leave it with you."

"Certainly, you can trust me to watch it and return it when you ask," he said eagerly, having heard of her husband and his treasures.

"Can I be perfectly sure that all will remain safely here?" she asked. Just then, as they had arranged, the poor man came into the room.

"Ah," said the kashi. "You want to be certain of my care and honesty. Well, here is just the way to show you. This poor man gave me 1000 tangas of his own to hold last year. He asked for them this morning, but I didn't recognise him. Now I shall return them, so you will know to trust me."

He turned to the poor man and gave him 1000 tangas. Then he reached out his hands for the woman's box. At once, her son raced in calling, "Mother! Mother! Father just returned with all the camels and goods."

"Wonderful," said the woman. "Now that my husband is home, he can watch the treasure. Thank you and forgive me for troubling you." Then she, her son, and the poor man walked out, leaving a very furious and disappointed kashi.

The man soon returned happily to his village and lived in peace, while the wise woman's family lived well, too, enjoying the arts and beauty of Tashkent for the rest of their days.

talk about

What does the phrase, 'meeting fire with fire' mean?

VISUAL ARTS

TEACHING PLATES

Plates in many parts of the world are decorated with lovely designs and colours. But a more unusual form of decoration is also found in the Muslim cultures of Central (and West) Asia: proverbs and sayings in elegant Arabic calligraphy have long graced plates and bowls there. The shapes of the English alphabet do not lend themselves as elegantly to a circular calligraphy as does Arabic, but students can try their best.

Materials

Traditional sayings
Paper and pencils

Method

❖ Write the sayings given below on the board or dictate to students.
❖ Describe the concept of a plate with writing on it (usually around the rim, but at times in the centre, too), meant to share wisdom.
❖ Have students make a large circle on their paper, and cut out if possible (or use paper plates if available).
❖ Ask students to choose one saying (or make another), and then try to write it, as artistically as possible, around the outer edge of the plate.
❖ Display the plates on the wall.

Source Material

Those content with their own opinion, run into danger.
He who speaks, his speech is silver, but silence is a ruby.
Prosperity and peace.
Planning before work protects you from regret.
He who professes the faith will excel.

CREATING FLAGS

When the new nations of Central Asia came into being, they each soon created a flag, an important symbol of national identity. Students can think about the importance of visual symbols as they create a new flag.

Materials

Slate and coloured chalk
Paper and colours or coloured cloth/paper scraps and paste
Description of new Central Asian flags

Methods

❖ Point to your national flag and see if students know what each symbol means. Explain that a flag communicates much about a nation.
❖ Share the descriptions below about several flags of the new Central Asian nations.
❖ Have students in small groups choose a town or city in your country and design a flag for it, based on the creative use of symbols and images (or they can design a new national flag!).
❖ Students can then make the flag by colouring on paper/slate, by pasting cloth scraps or coloured paper scraps on paper.

Source Material: Flags

Tajikistan Three horizontal stripes: red on top, white, green; gold crown with seven stars in centre to show state sovereignty, unity of people, and friendship among all nationalities

Kyrgyzstan Yellow sun on red background (for light, nobility, eternity) with 40 rays for the tribes led by Manas; in the sun is the peak of a traditional yurt (home)

Uzbekistan Three horizontal stripes: blue (top), white, green with two red thin stripes between; white crescent moon and 12 stars in upper left for rebirth of nation and the 12 signs of zodiac

GEOMETRIC PATTERNS

Many of the glorious monuments in Central Asia have beautiful tiled decorations: dancing across domes, carpeting courtyards, and enriching inner spaces, too. Students can experiment with tiles of different materials.

Materials

Tiles: cut from heavy paper, boxes, plastic, etc.

Method

❖ Ask students if they've seen pictures of the tile work on the Taj Mahal or another monument in their country. Share pictures of such work.

❖ Remind students how the effect of tile work is built up slowly from repetitions, and that the basic tile shapes are very simple: hexagons, octagons, squares, rectangles, crosses, and stars (eight-pointed ones were popular).

❖ Have students make tiles to work with: cutting or tearing colourful strips of various shapes but uniform sizes (so that they fit well together).

❖ Assign each pair or small group a surface to cover with their tiles: outside on ground/field/courtyard, inside on desks, tables, or floor.

❖ Let them experiment with designs and patterning as they create their tiled work. Since they are not gluing them, they can easily change patterns and correct mistakes. Enjoy the final products.

Note: Of course, tiles can also be glued down on paper for a lovely art project.

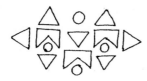

VERBAL/WRITTEN ARTS

SILK ROUTE STORIES

The trade routes collectively known as the Silk Route crisscrossed from China to the Middle East and Europe from around 200 BCE to 1500 CE. These active routes were first steps to globalisation, creating a valuable cross-pollination of art, technology, fashion, and ideas. The Silk Route opened doors and minds, sharing cultures and ideas. Give students a taste of this vital pathway.

Materials

Source material below; room decorations if desired

Method

❖ Introduce the Silk Route through materials you have, materials accessed on the net, and the trade goods below. Trace the common routes on a class map.

❖ Remind the students that besides goods, many stories were carried from East to West and West to East on the Silk Route.

❖ As a class, brainstorm the kinds of storytelling material that would be told along the way: folktales, legends of places, true stories of the wonders they'd seen, religious tales, songs, jokes, proverbs, riddles.

❖ Ask students to each prepare something short to share orally and to practice telling it to a partner.

❖ Set up your class as a *caravanserai*, a place fixed for a night halt along the way (drape a sari, light a lamp, sit around the floor). Take turns telling Silk Route tales!

Source Material: Popular items and their sources
Chang'an, China : silk cloth, grain, porcelain, herbs
Dunhuang, China: horses
Kashgar, China : dates, raisins, jade
Tashkent, Uzbekistan: horses, metal works, glass, musical instruments
Herat, Afghanistan: metal works, glassware, carpets, spices, camels
Baghdad, Iraq: gold, ivory, spices, cotton, pearls, gems
Damascus, Syria: silk

A DEBATE

'The Hawk' from Kyrgyzstan is a strange little tale. Its view of human nature is a rather grim one, thus the story can open up a fine discussion in your classroom.

Materials

The story

Method

❖ Have students read the story or read/tell it aloud to them.

❖ Ask them to tell you, in their own words, what the two characters feel about the world.

❖ See if they can make up some examples of actions that either animal might share, to support their view of the world.

❖ Discuss the two differing views with students and see if they believe in one or the other, and why.

Note: After a discussion, you could ask students to debate, each holding the worldview of a character. Or have students finish the discussion by making a drawing to show the two differing views.

SONGS/GAMES

KUMIS ALU (PICK UP THE COIN)

In older days, Central Asian young people played games on horses, since the horse was so much a part of the lifestyle. This game, adapted here, impressed Alexander the Great when he visited Central Asia, for he found it a great training for a warrior on horseback.

Materials

Handkerchief

Method

❖ Tell the students that this is a simple adaptation of an old game from parts of Central Asia. In the original game, a rider, galloping at full speed had to pick up a silver ingot off the ground; now a handkerchief is used.
❖ Explain that students will play the game running, not on horseback.
❖ Mark a start and finish line, quite far apart and put a handkerchief in the middle. Students then line up at start line and run quickly, trying to pick up handkerchief without slowing down. The fastest runner to pick it up wins.

LULLABIES

Around the world and across Central Asia, women have sung lullabies to their children. Enjoy these simple ones from Turkmenistan.

Materials

Lullaby words, written on board

Method

❖ Ask students to share a lullaby if they feel brave enough: one they use for a baby sibling, or one they remember their mother singing.
❖ Sing one of your own favourite lullabies if you can.
❖ Try the two lullabies from Turkmenistan, which have been rendered in English (they were originally in Turkmen). Have students read the words first, then add a gentle soothing, simple melody (that you make up or remember).

Source Material

He'll climb the hill, my sweet brother,
He'll wear a bell, my sweet brother.
When he sees his friends,
He'll smile, my sweet brother.

Will I not lull you to sleep?
Will Allah not accept my prayer?
Allah has created you,
Will He not become your friend?

NATURE/SCIENCE

GREED AND THE EARTH

'The Mountain of Gems' story highlights the problem of human greed. In this case, the gems were on top of the mountain, but often humans go after treasures inside the earth and damage it. In Central Asia, the greedy push to grow more cotton created one of the region's great ecological disasters: the changes in the Aral Sea. Students can examine their own region and seek developing problems to fight.

Materials

Research materials from the Internet, books, personal observations about regional (or national) environmental problems, especially those resulting from human greed.

Methods

❖ As a class, discuss some of the problems in nature caused by human greed and waste, whether by a person, a group, a company, etc.
❖ Identify a problem in your own region.
❖ Decide how your class could help to educate others about the problem, to work against those who are making the problem, or to help heal the

land if the damage is done. Think of letter campaigns, volunteer work, marches, exhibit at a festival/gathering, posters, etc.

❖ When you agree on a project, then gather any materials needed and get to work!

A FAVOURITE ANIMAL

The bards of Central Asia were renowned for their epics with generous description of fights, animals, characters, and settings. Students can use images, like a bard does, to describe a favourite animal.

Materials

Pen and pencil/slate and chalk
Excerpt from *Manas* quoted below

Method

❖ Ask students what kinds of storytelling they've seen, then introduce the rich art of epic storytelling across Central Asia (using material from other chapters in this book).

❖ Share the excerpt below from the long and very popular epic of *Manas*.

❖ Have the students react to the word picture painted of the horse that Manas so loved (see below). Ask the students to think of their favourite animal.

❖ Assign them each to write (or create to tell) a short paragraph about that animal. Encourage them to use vivid descriptions and comparisons as in *Manas*.

❖ Share them aloud, since many poems and stories are meant to be heard.

Source Material

When he ran, the black ground
Cracked layer after layer,
He didn't slip on the steep slopes,
He was no different at all
From a deer walking on cliffs.
... Raised in the wide pastures,
He was a pure-bred stallion
With iron lungs and copper wrists, (and in battle)
The rocks onto which he stepped crumbled,
Chunks of dirt the size of a small yurt flew,
His muscles moved with the grace of a sheep's,

His back was straight as a running rabbit's,
He opened his mouth really wide,
White foam mixed with blood
Splashed onto his chest...

(May: 1999, 70)

THINGS TO THINK ABOUT

CORRUPTION

Stories from every region might mention corruption, as '1000 Tangas' does in Central Asia, for it is a problem in various areas. Students can publicise the problems through political cartoons.

Materials

Samples of political cartoons from newspapers
Paper and pencil /slate and chalk

Methods

❖ Have students find political cartoons in local newspapers. Collect samples and share some that you find, too, to introduce the art form.

❖ As a class, discuss and list various types of corruption on local or national levels: taking bribes in an office, selling items without receipts to avoid taxes, a judge or politician being influenced by donations, etc.

❖ Working in pairs, the students then draw a cartoon together to show one of these problems or a similar type of corruption.

❖ Completed cartoons can be displayed in the school hall, drawn on a school chalkboard, printed in a newsletter, sent home to parents, and shared in various ways.

WOMEN LEADERS, A CLASS BOOK

Zarina, in the story of the same name, is a brave, strong female role model. There were strong queens during the Mongol times in Central Asia and strong Muslim queens in other parts of Asia. Students can learn more about strong women leaders, past and present, as they make a valuable class book.

Materials

Newspapers, books for research

Papers, pencils
String for binding, or stapler

Method

- ❖ Read the description of the Muslim Princess Raziyyah of India below, by Firishta, a 16th century historian. (see below) Then name various women leaders in your country, past and present.

- ❖ Working in pairs or individually, students can create pages on female leaders – in any field, on any level local to national. Each page can contain a drawing, facts of her life, any quotes if possible, and/or a short bio.

- ❖ Assign one student to create a cover collage on the theme.

- ❖ Assemble all the finished pages into one class book, with the cover in front, and adding a table of contents if desired. Stitch a binding or staple. Read and learn.

Source Material

"The Princess was adorned with every qualification required in the ablest kings, and the strictest scrutinisers of her actions could find in her no fault but that she was a woman. In the time of her father, she entered deeply into the affairs of government, which disposition he encouraged, finding she had a remarkable talent in politics. He once appointed her regent in his absence. When the emirs asked him why he appointed his daughter to such an office in preference to so many of his sons, he replied that he saw his sons giving themselves up to wine, women, gaming, and the worship of the wind (flattery): that therefore he thought the government too weighty for their shoulders to bear and that Raziyyah, though a woman, had a man's head and heart and was better than twenty such sons."
(Aghaie: 1998, 37)

Note: Firishta or Ferishta (c. 1560 – c.1620), given name Muhammad Qasim Hindu Shah was a Persian historian. In 1589 he moved to Bijapur where he spent the remainder of his life...writing a history of India. The first ten books are each occupied with a history of the kings of one of the provinces; the eleventh book gives an account of the Muslims of Malabar; the twelfth a history of the Muslim saints of India; and the conclusion treats of the geography and climate of India. Firishta is reputed as one of the most trustworthy of the Oriental historians, and his work still maintains a high place as an authority.
(http://en.wikipedia.org/wiki/Ferishta)

Stories and Activities
East Asia

Russian Federation

Sea of Japan

ULAAN BAATAR

North Korea

TOKYO

Kazakhstan

PYONGYANG

Japan

Mongolia

BEIJING

SEOUL

yrgyzstan

South Korea

Yellow Sea

People's Republic of China

East China Sea

India

TAIPEI

Nepal

Taiwan

Myanmar   Vietnam

South China Sea

THE REGION

IMAGES OF EAST ASIA INCLUDE the Great Wall, bamboo groves, elegant calligraphy, frenetic cities, mountain temples, the newest technology, and much more. The geography of the land is varied, from mountains to Steppes to sheltered islands, as are its religions/philosophies, from Shamanism to Buddhism, Confucianity, Islam, Shintoism and Christianity. East Asia is home to one of the world's longest continuous civilisations in China, dating from around 2500 BCE. After the powerful Qin conquered the other small states in the area, in 221 BCE, the empire of China began and continued for over 2000 years, moving through many dynasties and struggles. Numerous inventions and innovations came from China – paper, gunpowder, the compass, Confucian thought – and its influence was strongly felt in neighbouring Korea, Japan, and Vietnam.

Japan, another powerful East Asian country, was divided into smaller kingdoms in earlier times, but during the Yamato period grew as a united nation. Control of the state went from the refined court culture of the Heian time to the military rule of the Shoguns. Then Tokugawa Ieyasu started the Edo period with a strong central power that led to centuries of relative peace, with the warrior Samurai class ranking highest in importance. In 1853, however, arrived four U.S. steamships, thought by some Japanese to be "giant dragons puffing smoke". After months of negotiation, a treaty was signed in 1854 which opened Japan up for trade with the U.S., ending its long isolation.

Meanwhile, Korea found itself a "shrimp between two whales" as a Korean saying goes. Yet as kingdoms developed here, great accomplishments also followed: the construction of impressive Buddhist mountain temples, the invention of the world's first movable type, and the development of Hangul, a clear, scientific alphabet. Koreans were busy, too, fighting off invaders. One of the world's great military heroes, Admiral Yi Sun Shin, helped to resist the Japanese in the sixteenth century with the famous Turtle Boat, an early, awe-inspiring armoured boat.

However, all three were forced to open their doors in the nineteenth century to foreign powers, especially Great Britain and the U.S. Japan used the opportunity to develop scientific and industrial knowledge and went on to win wars against China and Russia, then to invade and rule harshly in Korea from 1910 to 1945.

China suffered through the Opium Wars, war with Japan, and internal struggle until, in 1949, Mao Zedong officially began a new, Communist chapter in Chinese history by forming the People's Republic of China. Decades

40

later, after a bloody Cultural Revolution, famines, and more, China has balanced its Communism with economic changes to become one of the world's largest economies.

Korea, after the Japanese left, found itself divided along the 38th Parallel. When the promised elections for unification didn't materialise, the North invaded the South in 1950. A tragic war followed, ripping families apart. There are still two Koreas today: South Korea, a major economic force in the world, and North Korea, which struggles under a strict regime.

Although the East Asian land of the Mongols hosted old cultures, the country of Mongolia is the newest democratic nation in East Asia. The land was the centre of the huge, powerful Mongol empire at first, but when that weakened, armies from China attacked again and again. The Manchus ruled oppressively over Mongolia for 200 years, from the late seventeenth century. Chinese influence continued until the twentieth century when Soviet troops offered help. The Soviet Union stayed closely aligned with Mongolia until 1990, when the Communists gave up power there.

Women have had some positions of power in East Asia, especially before the growth of Confucian influence in Korea and China, which restricted women's roles considerably. A number of East Asian women were well respected in the past, from the Korean Queen Sondok who ruled with wisdom and Lady Murasaki, the Japanese writer of the world's first novel, to the fierce Yang women warriors of China. Traditionally, Mongolian women, as nomads, had a strong position: they packed up yurt dwellings, made clothes and rugs, processed the crucial dairy and meat, and often tended to the sheep, leaving the men free to hunt or fight. And both men and women told stories . . .

. . . and its STORIES

Modern Chinese telling has its roots in the street storytelling popular centuries ago. Stories included *Journey to the West* featuring the beloved, mischievous Monkey; *Water Margins*, about several famous righteous outlaws; and *Romance of the Three Kingdoms* with its epic power struggles. The Chinese teller is accompanied at times by simple percussion instruments – bells, bamboo clappers, drums.

Around Suzhou and Shanghai, *pingtan* is popular; it includes *pinghua* telling without music and *tanci* with two tellers and their stringed instruments often sharing tales of romance. Sadly, the number of theatres and teahouses where this storytelling form can be found is dwindling. During the Cultural Revolution, many scholars were attacked, some tellers were imprisoned or banned from performing, some retrained to tell stories about revolutionary heroes. But in recent decades, with a loosening of some controls, storytellers can be heard satirising both society and the government, especially through the very popular comic storytelling form, *xiengshiang* (crosstalk), performed usually by two tellers.

In Korea, the sophisticated art of p'ansori demands years of practice. The form had its heyday in the nineteenth century, surviving into the twentieth century with a repertoire of five major stories. As the form faded, the movie 'S'opyonjae', a fictional account of an aging p'ansori teller, became an unexpected box-office hit in 1993 and brought new life to the art form.

In Japan, rakugo, a theatrical storytelling form popular since the sixteenth century and performed still in *yose* vaudeville theatres and on television, shares skills gained in long years of training. A master teller guides the beginner, usually a male, to polish skills of timing, improvisation, and characterisation. With a wave of his fan, a tilt of his head, a change of pose and voice, an accomplished rakugo teller creates convincing characters from the Edo period or draws laughter with modern stories of robots or baseball.

Other older forms, like *kodan* and *ryokyoku*, are fading, as did *gaito* (outdoor) *kamishibai* (paper theatre), popular from 1930 to 1960. Gaito kamishibai featured animated male tellers who told stories with handpainted sets of picture cards. In its heyday, some 30,000 players in Tokyo alone told tales using a tiny stage on the back of their bikes, after they'd sold snacks for their income. Today, many tellers in libraries and schools share newer published story sets of 12-16 cards, or create their own.

Temple legends or Buddhist stories are still told in some temples, and stories are passed on in some homes, and even in Hiroshima, where atomic bomb survivors tell their sad true stories to encourage peace. Storytelling in Japanese schools, libraries, and bookstores is growing, with the style often quiet, emphasising words not gestures. Storytellers such as the warm, talented writer/teller Matsuoka Kyoko of the Tokyo Children's Library, nourish the art form today: she teaches an annual course, produces a popular paperback series of tellable tales, *Ohanashi no Rosoku* (Story Candle), and encourages tellers throughout Japan.

Epics continue to be told in the wide open spaces of Mongolia. Heroes come alive as songs are sung to pass on pride, a sense of heritage, and an awareness of national identity. One of the longest epics in the world, the Tibetan tale of the hero, King Gesar of Ling (25 times as long as the *Iliad*) is still recited both in parts of Mongolia and among Tibetans.

China

This nation of diverse landscapes and ethnicities has the Gobi and Taklaman deserts vying for space with the Himalayas, the Steppes and the fertile alluvial plains of the Yangste and Hwang Ho rivers. The People's Repubic of China has made rapid strides in science, technology and commerce, while preserving its rich traditions of art and culture. It is credited with the invention of paper, silk and gunpowder. Chinese astrology, with its unique system of twelve zodiacs assigned animal names, is popular. Chinese opera, music, and martial arts still hold an important place as do the folk arts of puppetry, embroidery, paper-cutting

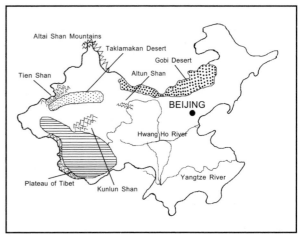

and folding, clay and paper toy-making, and storytelling. Included here are two small tales of worth. The first is a warm true story of a beloved father, by his daughter, journalist and educator Mabel Sieh in Hong Kong; the second a simple teaching tale that talks about horses, but applies just as well to humans!

My Father's Hands

MY FATHER'S HANDS were big and warm.

When I was small, I liked to play with his hands and feel the round, little hills around the edges. He liked to cover my little hands in his. And when he did it, I felt safe.

My father was hardworking and he often worked till late. I used to stand by the window looking down the street, waiting for him to come home. We lived on the top floor of an old building. There was no lift. I would wait until I saw his tall shadow moving towards the lamp-post, and I would run out the door and down the staircase, through eight flights of steps to greet him.

My father would always stand there for me. With a big daddy's smile, he took my hands and we walked to the little grocery store together. There were many things in the little grocery store and they had my favourite chocolates, too. All the chocolates were put in a round tall jar, where you could see them clearly. There were no fancy papers wrapping them or tin boxes covering them. There were round ones, square ones, funny shaped ones, dark ones, and light ones.

My father would let me take my time to pick my favourite pieces. I always loved the round ones. The shop lady put my chocolates in a little brown paper bag and placed it in my hand. I held my bag of chocolates in my right hand, and I held my father's hand in my left hand. And I walked home happily, feeling I had the whole world in my hands.

Years passed by and I grew up. I left the family and went to live in another country. Sometimes I would feel lonely, as we often do when we are on our own.

One year when things were very rough, I went home for the summer. When I walked in the door, my father ran out from the kitchen to greet me. He held my thin hands in his hands and said to me, "Come home anytime when you want to. Daddy will take care of you." Tears ran down my cheek as I felt the warmth and strength in his hands.

A clever builder makes a white house without bricks that later becomes cloth. What is it?

¡ɯɹoʍʞlᴉs A

43

Years passed by and my father became sick. He got a disease that made him forget the world. I went home again to see him. When I walked in the door, my mother came out to greet me. She told me that my father could not remember everybody anymore.

I went inside his bedroom where he was lying awake. I called him but there was no answering back. His hands were not moving to hold mine. I told him stories that I remembered: the window I was standing by, his shadow near the lamp-post, the little grocery store around the corner, the round jar of chocolates, the ones that I picked.

Then he looked at me with an uncertain gaze, as if he was wondering who I was. I took his hand and opened his palm. With my finger, I wrote my name on it, and I whispered, "Do you remember me?"

More years passed by. It was a cold winter when my father left this world. The funeral was as white as the first snow ever that fell on the ground. I stood next to my father's coffin to see him one last time. He was sleeping peacefully, his hands on his chest. I wished I could stand there forever.

For the last time, I took his hand, now thin and cold, and held it in mine. I thought about all the moments when his hands were holding mine.

His warmth, his trust, and his love will always be in my mind.

Two pieces of bamboo drive white ducks through a narrow door.

Chopsticks, rice !

True Worth

ONCE PRINCE MU OF QIN wished to find a successor to a valued advisor, Bo Li, who had watched over his horses for years. So he asked who should replace him.

"Many people can recognise good horses by their looks," Bo Li replied. "But a true judge of horses knows to see beyond the outer appearance, to the true character of the horse. My sons are people of modest ability, who can only judge by looks alone. So I would suggest my old friend, Juifang Gao. He can truly recognise inner quality in a horse."

The Prince soon called for Juifang Gao and sent him to find the most extraordinary horse in the world. He returned after three months and said he had found one.

"What is it like?" asked Prince Mu anxiously.

"It is a brown male," replied Juifang Gao. But his servant, who had also seen the horse, corrected him, saying, "No, sir, it was a black mare."

Prince Mu angrily called for Bo Li, then said, "How could you recommend such a fool. He doesn't even know whether the horse is black or brown, male or female!"

His old advisor sighed as he said, "Sir, his talent is indeed great. When he sees a horse, he only notices its spirit and its essential qualities, and forgets about the outer appearance. He remembers only the important things indeed." So the horse was sent for and it was truly a marvellous horse.

Two white walls, between them a yellow beauty.

An egg!

Japan

An island nation in the Pacific Ocean, Japan is often called the Land of the Rising Sun from the Kanji characters in its name meaning 'sun-origin'. It is an archipelago of over 3,000 islands. Mountainous, thickly vegetated, and vulnerable to earthquakes, Japan has the second largest economy in the world and is a technological trendsetter. Traditional arts include doll-making, lacquerware, pottery, *koto* playing, *kabuki* and *noh* drama. Its *manga* comics and *anime* animation are popular in many countries, as are its *sumo* wrestling and the martial arts of *judo*, *karate* and *kendo*. Shintoism and Buddhism, the main religious faiths, have given inspiration and a rich heritage of art to the country. The story below, set in an old temple, shares a part of ghostly Japan, with its many creatures: the *tengu* with long nose and wings, the *oni* monster with big teeth and horns, the mischievous water-loving *kappa*, and many more. A rakugo piece follows, but please imagine it told with the skill of a rakugo teller.

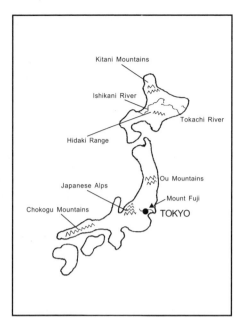

The Dark Temple

MUKASHI, MUKASHI... Long, long ago, one night a *samurai* passed a lonely, dark temple. He wanted to stay the night there, for it was late and he was tired. But some nearby villagers warned him away. "Too many strange things happen there, sir," they said. "And too many people go in and are never seen again." Yet the warrior only said, "*Daijobu*, I'm all right" and stomped proudly into the temple.

He looked calmly around then sat quietly on the floor. But suddenly, as he sat there, he heard:

"tsu tsu tsu, ka ra ka ra ka ra
tsu tsu tsu, ka ra ka ra ka ra"

Wondering at the strange sound, he opened the door and found a one-eyed stranger seeking shelter. The samurai kindly invited him in.

The stranger sat down, unfolded his cloth, and ate a rice ball. Then he offered one to the samurai, saying, "*Dohzo*, please." The samurai took it with an *arigato,* thank you. But when the samurai took the rice ball, all of a sudden it stuck to his forehead. He tried to remove it but his other hand stuck, too, and so did his knees. Soon he looked like a human ball as the old man rolled him out of the temple.

Tsugi no hi, the next day, another samurai came to the temple. He was warned away as well, but said bravely that he would stay. "Daijobu, daijobu," he told them. Yet soon, as he sat in the temple, he, too, heard:

"tsu tsu tsu ka ra ka ra ka ra
tsu tsu tsu, ka ra ka ra ka ra"

He opened the door, saw a one-eyed stranger, and invited him in. Again, the stranger unwrapped his cloth, ate a rice ball, and offered one to the samurai, "Dohzo." But the samurai refused saying, "*Ira nai*, I don't need it."

"Dohzo, dohzo," repeated the stranger, offering the rice ball again. Yet the samurai still repeated, "Ira nai."

It has six feet, yet it walks on four.

Man on horse!

Angry that the samurai still refused, the stranger suddenly threw the rice ball at him. It touched the man and turned into something large and clinging that covered his whole body. Surprised at the attack, the samurai pushed and pulled at the sticky net that now covered him. Struggling bravely, he finally freed his sword and plunged his sword into the stranger, who vanished at once:

"tsu tsu ka ra ka raaaaaaa"

The next day, all the villagers came to the temple and saw the samurai, drinking sake with the night's blood still on his clothes. Then they saw red drops, too, on the floor and followed a trail of blood out to a cave. Slowly the villagers looked in the cave and there they found. . .

. . . A HUGE, DEAD SPIDER, as large as an elephant, his enormous legs lifeless, his awful web still holding victims. And scattered all over his dark and terrible nest were bones, hundreds and hundreds of blood-stained human bones.

Tosa, so they say . . .

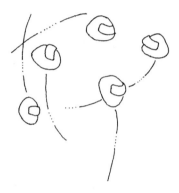

The Buns

ONCE IN OSAKA, a group of young men stood talking. All of a sudden, a man rushed up to them, looking quite terrified and crying, "Save me, save me!"

"What's wrong?" asked one man.

"The bun-seller is coming and I'm so, so scared of buns. Please help me. Don't let him see me."

The young men looked at each other, much amused. Then one man pointed to a broken-down hut and said, "Go hide in there." The man thanked them, ran quickly to it, and disappeared within. Soon after, a seller with boxes of buns rode by on a bike.

"Let us have a little fun," suggested the youngest man. "We'll buy all the buns and throw them at that coward."

The others laughed and rushed to buy buns. Each man held several buns as they formed a circle around the hut. Then, one at a time, each tossed a bun through the holes and windows. Every time a bun went in, they heard an "AAAHHH!" or a "Help!" or some such satisfying noise. At last all the buns were gone, all thrown in with many a frightened sound heard in reply. But suddenly, it was too quiet. No sound came from the house. The young men now looked very worried.

"Perhaps we went too far," said one.

"I do hope we didn't scare him to death," whispered another.

"We'd better check and see if we can save him," suggested the bravest man. Slowly he went toward the old door. Still no sound could be heard inside. With his heart beating too fast, he finally pushed open the door and looked inside.

There sat the man afraid of buns. But he didn't look scared at all now. He looked most contented and very full. With a smile, he brushed off the last crumb from his mouth. "Ah, that was most delicious," he said looking up at them. "Thank you. Now, I'm so, so scared of a good, hot cup of tea."

North and South Korea

The Democratic People's Republic of Korea (North) and the Republic of Korea (South) were formed in 1953 after three bloody years of war. Although North Korea now follows a Communist path, both countries share a common Buddhist and Confucian heritage, with a strong move towards Christianity recently. The Korean *Hangul* alphabet is one of the most phonetic and well-designed, created during the reign of King Sejong. Korea's musical heritage includes lively mask dances, vibrant percussive sounds of farmers' music, and the elegance of the *gayageum* (zither). *Taekwondo*, a popular martial art, originated in South Korea and is standard military training in a country which is a major economic and technological force. The Korean peninsula has an 8,640-km coastline, with some 3,569 islands adjacent to it. It has mountains and rivers with a history of too many wars and invasions. The two stories share the wisdom of Korea; the second features an important character in Korean lore – the secret royal inspector.

The Magic of Cloth

LONG AGO, IN KANGHWA, there was a soldier who hated to fight. So he journeyed to the mountains and studied Taoist magic for some time, but kept it his secret.

One morning, he sat with his wife in their small home and watched her sew. But she was in a bad mood that day. With a frown, she picked out pieces of bright cloth to stitch into a *chogakpo* quilt. With quick, angry stitches she pieced them together. Although the chogakpo looked lovely, she was unhappy with her work, and the soldier wondered why.

He wanted to cheer her up, but what could he do? Ahh! All at once, he knew. He reached over and picked up several pieces of the most colourful reds, yellows, and greens. Placing them in his hands, he blew on them. All of a sudden, they turned into brilliant butterflies that circled round the small room.

His wife looked up in surprise. With wide eyes, she watched the magical butterflies. She saw the red of pepper strings, the green of new rice fields, the yellow of soft melons – all on butterfly wings. A smile soon spread across her face, and then she laughed out loud in delight. The couple watched the wondrous butterflies as they swooped and shimmered, glittering in the sunlight.

Finally, the soldier opened his hand again and placed his palm up. The butterflies quickly flew down and landed on the hand. Their wings whispered to the wind, then slowed down in farewell. Gently, he closed his hand over them. After a moment, he opened it.

In the hand now were only the lifeless pieces of cloth, which he gave back to his wife. But now, as she sewed her quilt, she sewed with pleasure, happy again. The sound of a soft song floated from her mouth as her needle danced in and out. And while her fingers moved swiftly, she thought of those wonderful butterflies, and stitched their beauty and grace into her chogakpo.

Gold inside,
silver outside.

An egg.

The Cows

ONE DAY, THE FAMOUS SECRET ROYAL INSPECTOR, Hwang Hui, was travelling in disguise to inspect the country. He wished to find out what was good and what was bad, to help the king make a better land. In the shadow of a cloud-tipped mountain range, he came upon a farmer standing in his field. Near him grazed both a black cow and a white cow.

Curious about the two very different types, Hwang Hui thought, "I shall find out which is the best cow and tell the king so that all farmers can prosper." So he called out to the farmer, "Sir, which cow is the better cow?"

The old farmer was some distance away, but still close enough to shout an answer. However, he did not. He simply started to walk to Hwang Hui, but slowly as if in pain.

Hwang Hui felt bad watching the old man walk so painfully. He cried out, "Just call out and tell me which cow is better. I can hear." But the farmer was still silent as he walked on.

"Please, sir, you can speak now, I can hear," cried Hwang Hui, trying to stop the farmer's aching feet. Yet the farmer simply walked on in silence. At last, he stood right next to the inspector. Even then he did not speak out. He bent forward and whispered, "The black one is better, sir."

"Thank you for your reply," said Hwang Hui who was puzzled by the man's actions. "But you could have called out to me. You didn't have to walk all the way here to whisper your answer."

The old farmer leaned over again and whispered, "I couldn't shout out loud, sir. Animals have feelings, too, don't they?"

talk about
Feelings. What are they about? And why do they matter?

Mongolia

The Mongols gained fame in the 13th century when, under Genghis Khan (1162-1227), they conquered a huge Eurasian empire. After his death the empire was divided into several powerful Mongol states; the Mongols eventually retreated to their original Steppes homeland in present-day Mongolia, which later came under Chinese rule. Mongolia won its independence in 1921 with Soviet backing, a Communist regime was installed in 1924, two parties ruled at different times after that, and a coalition government was created in 2004. It is one of the coldest countries of the world, and home to much of the Gobi desert.

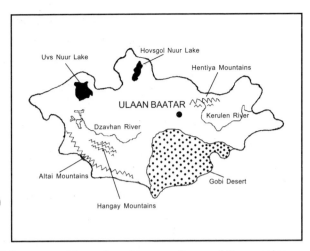

Over the years, the wide open spaces of Mongolia called for heartfelt song and for epics of heroes. Some of these epics, like that of King Gesar, were often told to the sounds of the horse-head fiddle, *morin khuur* in Mongolian. This poignant tale tells how the instrument came to be.

A Wondrous Fiddle

LONG AGO, ON THE WIDE, OPEN PLAINS of Mongolia, there dwelt a young boy named Suho. He lived with his grandmother in a warm yurt and helped to rear the few sheep they owned. Although the two had little wealth, they felt blessed with the life they had.

Every day, Suho took the sheep to graze. As he sat and watched them, he sang songs and dreamt of galloping fiercely over the plains. One evening, though, he didn't return at the usual time. As the dark deepened, his grandmother grew very frightened. She called to others nearby and asked their help. Soon, the night was lit by the torches of many searching for a young boy, who might be hurt, deadly hurt.

As one after another returned with no news, the grandmother's fears grew. Then suddenly she heard a beloved sound as Suho called to her, holding something in his arms.

"Look, grandmother," he cried. "Look what I found." And he showed her a beautiful, white foal. "She was lying on the ground when I found her. So tiny and weak. I waited and waited for her mother to return, but she never came. I was afraid the wolves would get her tonight. The poor thing is all alone. May I keep her and raise her?"

"Ahh," said the grandmother, crying happy tears now. "Yes, yes indeed."

Many carefree days followed as Suho and the foal grew together. Every sunrise, Suho fed her grass then together they watched the sheep. Every evening, the two returned happily to the yurt. Soon, the colt had turned into a strong white horse. Now, Suho proudly rode the animal at dawn and dusk and the two seemed as one. Suho felt freer than the wind when he galloped across the plains with his horse, his best friend.

All his friends watched in envy as Suho's white horse simply sailed past them. Then, one day, news came of a great contest in a nearby city. The rider with

On one side of a river are some sheep tended by a man. Across the river is another flock. One shepherd called across, "If you give me one of your sheep, I'll have twice as many as you have."
The other replied, "If you give me one sheep, we'll have an equal number."
How many sheep were in the two herds?

7 and 5.

49

the fastest horse would marry the governor's daughter. Suho's friends urged him to go and try. So he set out.

Soon, he reached the grand city and marvelled at the fine stone buildings there. The two then moved on to the contest field. They stood in place with all the others, in front of a splendid tent sitting under bright banners. The race began and Suho at once took the lead. Faster and faster the two flew until they almost vanished. There was no doubt who had won. Suho was summoned to claim his reward.

But when the governor saw not a strong warrior or a rich nobleman but only a poor shepherd, he refused to give his daughter.

"Give him three silver coins for the horse," he said. "Then send him away."

"Sir," cried Suho. "I didn't come to sell my best friend. I came for your promised reward."

"Stupid boy!" roared the ruler. "I'll give you a reward!" And he ordered his guards to beat the boy and to take his horse. Soon, Suho found himself alone, in great pain, with blood all around and no sign of his beloved horse. After some time, his friends saw him and gently carried him home.

With the kind care of his grandmother, Suho's body soon healed. But his spirit would not. He missed his horse so much that he could hardly eat, could barely sleep. When he did close his eyes, he dreamt only of his best friend. Time passed but did not heal the boy.

Meanwhile, the cruel governor one evening decided to ride the grand horse. The horse was brought with a rich saddle on it. Servants held on tightly as he mounted. But as soon as that greedy man got on the horse, she reared up and threw him to the ground. Then the horse raced off like the wind.

"Catch her or kill her!" roared the ruler in a rage. Guards on horseback raced after her, their arrows flying. Several of the arrows hit the horse, but they did not stop her.

That night, as Suho tried to sleep, he suddenly heard a sound outside — a panting, sighing sound. He pulled up the flap of the yurt and looked out. There stood his horse, very weak, with arrows sticking out of her sides, and blood flowing down. Suho sobbed as he ran to the horse and hugged her tightly. His grandmother soon came out and the two soothed the horse, placing healing herbs on her.

But it was too late. Although the horse had found the strength to return to her friend, she had not the strength to live. In the morning, Suho held onto his beloved horse, begging her not to die. Painful moments passed but at last, the horse shivered and fell silent.

Suho's grief now was greater than before, for he knew he'd never see his beloved friend again. That night, though, when his eyes somehow closed in sleep, he had a dream. In the dream, he saw his horse and the horse spoke.

"Suho, my friend," she said. "You must not weep for me. I will tell you how you can best remember me. Tomorrow, take my body and carefully remove the hide, sinews, and bones. Clean them well and put them together to make an instrument with strings and a bow. Carve the shape of a horse head on the top of the fiddle. Then, whenever you play it, you will think of me. I will be near you and hear you. We'll be together again."

The next morning, Suho did as the horse instructed. He worked carefully and took many days. He took special care to carve the head of his beloved horse, crying at times as he worked. But at last, he gazed on a beautiful, horse-head fiddle. Slowly, he started to play it. And slowly, slowly he forgot his great sorrow. Soon, many gathered to hear his heartfelt songs. He shared his music eagerly, for every time he touched the horse-head fiddle, he remembered his horse and sang to her, too.

After a while, others made horse-head fiddles and shared their lovely notes. Lonely nights on the plains were filled richly now with a new sound. And in this way, the memory of a faithful horse was carried on and on through the power of song.

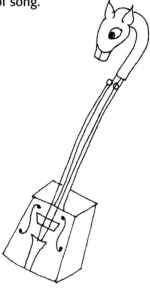

talk about

Who is a friend?
What does friendship
mean to you?

Taiwan

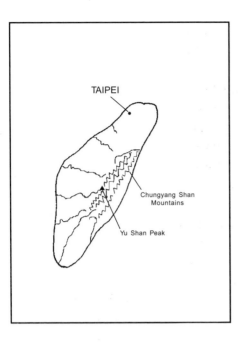

TAIPEI

Chungyang Shan Mountains

Yu Shan Peak

The Republic of China is commonly known as Taiwan or Chinese Taipei. This small island, mostly covered by mountains and dense tropical and sub-tropical vegetation, has a population comprising native Taiwanese of Hakka and Gujian descent, some indigenous people, and Chinese emigrants. A long history of foreign occupation has left indelible imprints on Taiwan's culture: the influence of East Asia is seen in its fine arts, folk traditions, and popular culture. The primary languages of communication are Mandarin and Taiwanese (both the Hakka and Minnan dialects), while English is a common second language in schools. Economically, the country is one of Asia's smaller tigers, and it is justly proud of its traditions, including its many local legends. This small legend explains the name of the mountain Ban Pin Shan ('a half') in Taiwan as it also gently teaches.

Ban Pin Shan

LONG YEARS AGO in southern Taiwan, there was a large, finely shaped mountain with a small village nestled at its base. One morning, an old, white-haired man, in worn and tired clothes, came to sell dumplings in that village. The people there smelled the delicious aroma then listened to his words with surprise: "Fine dumplings for sale. One for ten coins, two for twenty, three for free!"

"The man is mad," said one of the villagers as the man repeated: "One for ten, two for twenty, three for free!" Finally, someone decided to test the strange offer. At once, the old man gave him three huge, delicious dumplings and would not take any coins. Soon the other villagers began to eat eagerly, and each one ordered three, so no one paid. After some time, all the man's dumplings were gone. He smiled, waved, and walked off.

Just then, a villager who had enjoyed the dumplings glanced at the mountain and cried, "Look, the mountain looks strange today. As if it's missing something." The others didn't listen and talked instead about the incredible dumplings and their amazing price! They all agreed that the old man was truly stupid, and they wondered what he used to make the special dumplings.

The next day, the old man came again, crying, "Fine dumplings for sale. One for ten coins, two for twenty, three for free!"

At once, everyone ran to the old man. Quickly they ordered three dumplings each. With big grins, they stuffed the big dumplings in their mouths and walked off delighted at the bargain. Soon, all the dumplings were gone and the old man walked off without a coin.

On the third day, he came again, cried out the same

prices, and started to give the dumplings away, for everyone wanted "three for free." But then, all of a sudden, a voice called out, "Sir, I'd like to buy just one."

Shaking his head, the old man searched and saw that the voice belonged to a poorly dressed young man. The old man stared at him and asked, "Didn't you hear? My dumplings are one for ten coins, two for twenty, or three for free. Why pay for one when you can get three for free?"

"I heard you," replied the young man. "But I feel sorry that you carry a heavy load everyday, yet make no money. I want to help, and I have enough money to pay for one dumpling." When they heard those words, many of the villagers suddenly felt very greedy and much ashamed.

"Ahhh! At last, I've found the right person," cried the old man. "I am the god of the mountain. But I came in disguise, with magic dumplings made from the mountain's mud, seeking the right student. And you alone have a kind, caring heart. You will be my pupil, for I have powers to teach you." Now everyone understood. They watched sadly as the young man followed the mountain god and the two disappeared. They ran to look at the dumplings still left. But all they found was a pot full of mud.

"Look," cried a villager, pointing to the mountain. Everyone looked and saw that much earth was now missing from their mountain. It looked like only half a mountain now. The villagers felt great regret and shame. And from that time on, the mountain was called Ban Pin Shan and whenever they looked at it, the villagers remembered both their own greed and the young man's kind heart.

talk about

Our wants are our needs and our needs are our wants... On second thoughts, are they?

VISUAL ARTS

TINY KAMISHIBAI

In Japan for almost a century, picture storytelling cards have been used to share a range of tales (see Overview). Students really enjoy making their own sets, then sharing them.

Materials

A story to share
Eight cards the same size (backs of greeting cards work well, or blank index cards, unless you want a bigger size)
Pencil and colour markers

Method

❖ Have students choose a story to illustrate, one with action that can be divided into eight scenes.
❖ Ask students to line up their cards and to roughly sketch out the main scenes. Have them use any of the following to add visual variety: close-ups of characters or setting; far away shots of setting; views from different angles: top, side, front, back; borders – for certain scenes, not each one; a picture of just part of a character: hand, foot, etc.
❖ Check their rough sketches for variety and interest.
❖ Next have students colour in and finish their drawings, making sure that figures are large enough to be seen.
❖ When they're done, students should number cards then practice telling story with partners and in small groups.

Note: Kamishibai can be made on larger cards, e.g. A4 or larger, but a stiff paper/card must be used so that they can be held and won't fall over.

KOREAN FAN DRAWING

Lovely paper fans are found throughout East Asia: both folding types and flat ones. Both shapes were often beautifully decorated in Korea, sometimes with poems written on them. Students can make a fan and then decorate it with a scene from a story.

Materials

Korean fan
Paper of any type and size for fans
Colours

Method

❖ Draw fan shape, shown alongside, on the board for others to draw, or enlarge and make copies for each student.
❖ Have students choose a scene from one story and draw it on the fan.
❖ Finished fans can be nicely displayed on walls or hung from lines, etc.

OMAKE

For years, the Japanese have had a delightful idea: combining tiny toys or books with sweets. This *omake* tradition has been enjoyed by generations: the tiny toys included small cars/trucks, tiny books, little models, and much more. Some of the many designs are displayed in a lovely, small museum of toys in Osaka, Japan. Students can make their own adaptations for some sweet fun.

Materials

Any type of scrap material to make tiny toys
Sweets
Newspaper to wrap both together (or small boxes – matchboxes, etc. if available)

Method

❖ Tell students about this tradition. Ask if they know of any similar ideas.
❖ Have them bring in materials to make a tiny toy of any kind (you can also have some materials on hand).
❖ Challenge each student to make a toy about the size of a flat ping pong ball.
❖ When each student finishes, s/he can be given a sweet and a piece of paper (or little box). The two are then wrapped together (the wrapping can be decorated if desired).
❖ The omake can be taken home to give to a sibling or exchanged with other students.

CALLIGRAPHY

The art of calligraphy developed in East Asia, as it did in West and Central Asia. The elegant Chinese characters are used in China and Japan today (although Japanese add the letters of their own alphabet too), while in Mongolia and Korea there is a trend to use their own fine alphabets and/or characters. The Chinese characters are especially nice for students to work with, for some are types of pictographs.

Materials

Copy of characters below
Paper and pencil, or black ink/paint and thin brushes if available

Method

❖ Show students the Japanese *kanji* characters below, and their meanings.
❖ Students can then copy each shape several times, to make the shapes smooth.
❖ Characters can be shared in any way you dream up.

SUNDAY
SUN
NICHI

SATURDAY
EARTH
DO

THURSDAY
TREE
MOKU

MONDAY
MOON
GETSU

FRIDAY
GOLD
KIN

WEDNESDAY
WATER
SUI

TUESDAY
FIRE
KA

HANGING PROVERBS

In East Asia, banners were often used during wars, during worship, or for decoration. Help students make a banner and fill it with favourite Asian proverbs.

Materials

One large piece of paper per small group
Colours and pens
Proverb list below

Method

❖ Write the proverbs on the board.
❖ Ask students to share a proverb or saying that they heard while growing up.
❖ Read the East Asian proverbs on the board.
❖ Divide students into small groups and give each group a large paper and colours/pens.
❖ Ask students to choose some of the East Asian proverbs or to use some that they know and to make a colourful poster/display/collage with the proverbs.
❖ Remind them that they can also write the proverb on another sheet and paste it on, or make a drawing to illustrate the proverb, etc.
❖ Display proverb banners on the wall, for all to enjoy.

Source Material

A book is a garden, carried in your pocket.
A book, tight shut, is but a block of paper.
China

Even a sheet of paper weighs less
if four hands lift it.
A dead tree blooms again.
Korea

One kind word can warm three winter months.
Even monkeys fall from trees.
Japan

A horse released can be caught, a word released, never.
Stay alive and one day you will drink from a golden cup.
Mongolia

Better than the young man's knowledge is the old man's experience.
Tibet

SONGS/GAMES

BEATING THE DRUM

Games of all kinds are enjoyed by young and old in China. Here is a classroom adaptation of a traditional Chinese drinking game, that is a fun test of skill.

Materials

Drum or any surface to drum on
One large (non-breakable) tumbler of water

Method

❖ The class (or part of class, if class is too large) sits in a circle, with one student apart, his back to the group.
❖ That student starts to drum on a surface, varying his speed. As he drums, the tumbler of water is passed from one person to the next, reflecting the speed of the drumming.
❖ Water must be passed without spilling. The student who spills water is out. Game continues until the water is gone or one person is left.

DRAWING SONGS

Japanese children have for many years enjoyed singing a song while drawing a picture. Share this delightful example while chanting/saying the song. If you want, students can go on to try to make their own drawing songs.

Materials

Song below
chalkboard / slate or paper for students

Method

❖ Learn the design and practice chanting each part as you draw that part. Make sure the drawing and the chanting/singing match, and that one doesn't get ahead of the other!
❖ Now take your chalk and 'perform' the song.
❖ Teach it slowly to students as they work on slates or paper.

Note: You can challenge older students to make up a simple drawing song/story, keeping the final drawing a surprise, if possible.

Source Material

Rokuchan ga		Little sis
mame kute		Ate a bean
omimi naga naga		Long, long ears
usagisan		Mr Rabbit

NATURE/SCIENCE

ANIMAL TRAITS

In traditional Chinese thought, the dragon combined the traits of various animals. Share the list of traits below. Then challenge students to create their own animals.

Materials

List below
Slate/paper

Method

❖ Ask students what they know about dragons.

Then share the list below, naming just the animals and asking students to guess which part would be useful for a dragon and why.
❖ As a class, or in partners/small groups, have students create another composite animal: defining traits from 'donor animals', then giving the new animal a name, diet, setting, and drawing the animal, if they wish.
❖ Share the creations.

Source Material

Dragon is made from: head of a camel, whiskers of a catfish, horns of a deer, eyes of a rabbit, ears of a water buffalo, feet of a tiger, neck of a serpent, belly of a frog, scales of a carp, claws of a hawk.

THE FEEL OF THE SEASONS

Although most people enjoy the change of seasons across East Asia, the Japanese are especially sensitive to the differences, and their poetry reflects this. Those writing short haiku poetry in Japan often consult *A Dictionary of Haiku*, which lists the many images of each season in haiku. Students can make their local seasonal dictionary.

Materials

List of images below
Paper and pencil

Method

❖ Share some of the typical Japanese images of the seasons written below, telling students that these are only some of the seasonal plants popular in Japanese stories and poetry.
❖ On the board, write the different seasons found in your area, talk briefly about the various plants, animals, games, activities, etc. found in the different seasons.
❖ Have students make a small Japanese style folding book, by folding a narrow, long paper in a fan style back and forth.
❖ Put the title on first page, then a name of season on each page inside.
❖ Students then write and draw as many images/symbols of each season as possible.

Source Material

Some seasonal plants (from *A Dictionary of Haiku*):
Spring plants: apple blossom, cherry blossom, iris, dandelion, rhododendron, willow, plum blossom

Summer plants: daisy, foxglove, lotus, peach, rose, strawberry

Autumn plants: acorn, apple, chrysanthemum, cottonwood, fallen leaves, maple, persimmon

Winter plants: bare tree, birch, cedar, withered grass, pine

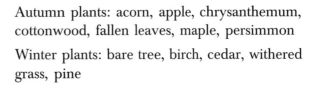

THINGS TO THINK ABOUT

PEACE STRATEGIES

The countries of East Asia have often been at war with each other and stories/writings about war strategies abound. Now it's time for peace. When the Chinese invaded Tibet in the 1950s, great pain was given, yet Tibet's spiritual leader, the Dalai Lama, felt compassion and not rage toward the invaders. Share his wisdom and help students make a book of peace, not war, strategies.

Materials

Excerpt below to read
For class book, have paper/pencil for all
For class list, just use chalk board

Method

❖ Discuss the areas of war and fighting in your nation and the world.
❖ Read the comment by the Dalai Lama below.
❖ Ask students to think of what tools are needed to make peace and not war.
❖ For class list: have them dictate ideas for 'peace strategies' (forgiveness, talking, compromise, etc.) for you to write on board.
❖ For class book: each student draws a picture of a 'peace strategy' and/or writes strategy below. Assemble all papers and bind into a book.

Source Material: (about a Tibetan monk, Lopon-la, who was put in prison for 18 years by the Chinese)

"...When he finally free, he came to India. For twenty years, I did not see him. But he seemed the same. Of course looked older. But physically ok. His mind still sharp after so many years in prison. He was still same gentle monk. He told me the Chinese forced him to denounce his religion. They tortured him many times in prison. I asked him whether he was ever afraid. Lopon-la then told me:

'Yes, there was one thing I was afraid of. I was afraid I may lose compassion for the Chinese' " (Chan: 2004, 47).

DON'T BREAK THE SPIRIT

The nomads of Mongolia have much wisdom earned from years of living in a challenging environment. This song and the sayings are used to help encourage losers in a contest to keep going – a good reminder for students everywhere.

Materials

Sayings, song and description below

Method

❖ Locate Mongolia on the map, if necessary.

❖ Introduce the sayings and song on the idea of losing.

❖ Discuss the concept involved: that losing is not an ending and that the loser can be consoled and encouraged.

❖ As a class or in small groups, make up a small song or saying that could be used when students lose. You might even make some prizes for the losers, not the winners, in a class game.

Source Material

The last rider to finish a big horse race in Mongolia is awarded a special, lavish prize as this song is sung. The prize reflects the wisdom of the nomads who wanted to encourage even the race losers to try again, for as their sayings go, 'Better to break one's spine than the spirit' and 'A man fails seven times and rises eight times.'

Because of a foolish owner,
the reins were too short...
The rider was too young, and the whip too short.
Too many sand dunes happened on the way,
As well as many hills and ravines.
As always there were obstacles.
And though the jockey tried hard,
To overcome all of them, still too many remained.
The young colt lagged behind all
But next year,
the rider will be ahead of 10,000 horses.
(mongoliatoday.com/issue/7/tales.html)

Stories and Activities
South Asia

THE REGION

ACROSS THE REGION OF SOUTH ASIA, over the centuries, have travelled conquerors, traders, saints, monks, and countless others of various faiths. India, the largest country in the region, is largely Hindu (as is Nepal); it is surrounded by the faith of Islam in Pakistan, Afghanistan and Bangladesh, and the Buddhism of Sri Lanka. Although fighting has erupted at times over issues of religion or identity, there have also been long years of peaceful co-existence; many South Asians, from various backgrounds, from Emperor Asoka to the Pushtun peace hero Badshah Khan, have worked for harmony.

Many parts of this mixed region were colonised, largely by the British. Their rule produced disastrous economic effects and left a legacy of problems in education, national self-worth and identity, among others. At last, after centuries of struggle and much hardship, with the inspiration of heroes like Tipu Sultan, Rani Lakshmi Bai, Mohammad Ali Jinnah, Mahatma Gandhi, and many others, independence was achieved in 1947. Pakistan was created as the British pulled out in 1947; later, that country divided itself again, when East Pakistan – which had a different cultural background and language – rebelled to become Bangladesh.

It is a region blessed with a great range of geographic features and climates, from the incredible majesty of the Himalayan mountains to the deserts of Sindh and Rajasthan, great rivers like the sacred Ganga, the hills of central Sri Lanka, and the waterways of Bangladesh. Animals from tigers and peacocks to rhinos and deer are found in the area, some in wildlife sanctuaries that are popular tourist attractions.

The history of the region is a rich one; it was home to one of the world's oldest civilisations – the Indus Valley – that had complex planned cities, with granaries and even household toilets. As centuries passed, countless small kingdoms grew, at times fighting, at other times co-existing. Waves of invaders from Alexander of Macedonia on through the Mughals down to Western powers came as well. Some areas, protected by nature through mountain ranges or water, managed to remain outside the worst of the wars, while others were open to a range of attackers. Earlier, powerful empires in the region included the Guptas, the Mauryas, the Cholas, among others.

Today, the region has a mixed economy: information technology has made huge advances in India, while some villages in the region don't have electricity. Many South Asians still struggle with poverty, and some very innovative ways of self-help and rural development have started here. The micro-banking ideas of Grameen Bank in Bangladesh have provided help and loans to over six million members from the poorest sections, including some who have to beg for a living.

The visual art of South Asia is a collage as well – from the awesome Buddhas of Bamiyan in Afghanistan, destroyed by the Taliban, to the huge temples of South India, the Mughal forts and palaces in Pakistan, the gaily painted rickshaws of Bangladesh, the Tibetan thangkas found in Nepal, the ancient city of Sigiriya in Sri Lanka, and the modern calligraphy of the Maldives. Literature was an oral art for centuries, too, and the region remains rich in storytelling, as you will see in the pages that follow.

. . . and its STORIES

For centuries, caravans going East and West would meet, and storytellers would exchange news and tales in the Storyteller's Bazaar of Peshawar. It still exists today, but is full of traffic and noise, with no live tellers in sight. However, their voices are still heard, for storytelling cassette tapes sell briskly, helping listeners to remember the past and tellers to find new audiences.

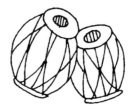

Today in Pakistan, the stories of refugees are shared, along with tales of the Prophet and other teaching tales from Islam. Ballad styles of story singing are still found, but they face competition from the modern world. The Baloch people of Pakistan, Afghanistan and Iran used storytelling frequently in the past. When a boy was born, "a special session of epic recitation would be arranged and male elders of the family invited...and a male elder or someone else would recite heroic epics for three or seven nights. This was the first lesson the newborn boy would receive from the elders of his family, who expected him to behave accordingly and to follow in the footsteps of past Baloch heroes". (Badalkhan: 2003, 229) Stories were also told in homes, later, on winter nights during Ramzan. However, this is no longer true. As Badalkhan sadly writes, "One can say without hesitation that oral tradition is now a dying art in Balochistan...Times are changing rapidly (with satellite television and the rise of fundamentalist Islam that forbids singing) and it is unlikely that Balochi oral traditions, such as storytelling sessions, can survive even a couple of decades from now...many of these forms have not been collected and preserved." (Badalkhan: 2003, 232)

Across India, some storytelling forms are also in danger while others still draw crowds. Modern tellers such as Jeeva Raghunath of Chennai and the tellers of Kathalaya in Bangalore try to promote the art form in schools, bookstores, festivals and wherever they can.

Meanwhile, traditional forms are many and varied (see *World of Indian Stories* for more detailed information on Indian storytelling traditions). In Rajasthan, the intricately painted phad scroll is set up by the bhopa teller, who then weaves nightlong tales, most often of the hero Pabuji. Another painted marvel in Rajasthan is an ingenious storytelling box. The kavad has a number of door panels, painted in vivid colors, which unfold to share stories of the gods. In West Bengal, the narrow vertical scroll, the pata, is still used to tell both traditional myths and modern stories: the French government even sponsored one made on the French Revolution! In the state of Maharashtra, the stirring mixture of song and narrative in the kirtan form attracts hundreds to hear stories of gods, saints and devotees. Several centuries ago, this form travelled from Maharashtra to southern Tamilnadu, evolving into the sophisticated harikatha style.

Musical storytelling forms in India are too many to list. In the far south, the villupattu style is one of the more unusual ones. Burra katha troupes in Andhra Pradesh state usually have a main teller, a questioning assistant, and a drummer who plays the burra drum. Amidst the rich landscape of Kerala state flourish a number of storytelling styles such as Chakyar koothu, performed only in temples, and ottan thullal, a more lively form of telling. Kathaprasangam of Kerala is a secular style that developed in the twentieth century to popularise local literature and to challenge societal problems of caste, corruption, and inequality.

Afghanistan

A landlocked country and a focal point for trade, Afghanistan has attracted invaders from the Achaemenid Persians and the Greeks to the British, Soviets and Americans. The Hindu Kush mountains divide the northern provinces from the rest of this rugged country that has seen too much struggle, both among proud, local clans and with outsiders. The majority of people in this ethnically mixed nation are Pashtun, with Persian and Pashto the official languages and Islam the predominant religion. Afghan carpets are an admired craft and classic Persian poetry still plays an important role in Afghan culture, where literacy levels remain low. A rich musical tradition, suppressed for many years but recently revived, includes folk music played on *ghaychak*, dutar, flute and cymbals, and a classical vocal style with formats such as *raags*, ghazals and *taraanas*. A long tradition of storytelling includes tales of the favourite trickster, Abu Khan.

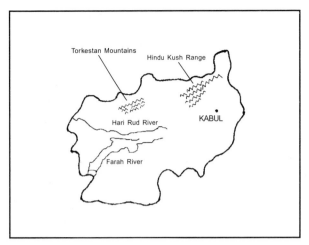

The Flies

ONE NIGHT THE EMIR OF HERAT had a strange dream – that there was a bag of gold buried under Abu Khan's house. The next morning, the emir sent his guards to dig up Abu Khan's house, seeking the gold.

Abu Khan was out walking while this took place. When he returned, he found his wife sobbing, surrounded by bricks and pieces of his home. The guards had not found any gold, but they had badly damaged Abu Khan's house.

"What can we do for justice?" cried his wife. "Who will punish the greedy emir?"

Abu Khan gazed around in thought and suddenly said, "Make some fine *biryani* and I will see what is possible." His wife, wondering how he could eat at such a time, went to the kitchen that was luckily still standing and prepared some sweet-smelling biryani, with spices and good meat. She placed it on the floor in front of Abu Khan.

He didn't eat even a handful, though. He just sat and let many, many flies settle on it. When it was covered with flies, he carefully put a cloth over it, capturing the flies within. Then he went to the emir's great hall.

"I have a grievance, sir," he said. "Some strangers came to my house uninvited and did damage. I wish to punish them."

The emir liked to seem a fair man, even though he wanted to protect himself. He spoke slowly, "And who were these strangers?"

With a flourish, Abu Khan took off the cloth and flies darkened the room.

"Here they are, sir," he said. "I wish your permission to kill any fly I see from now on."

Laughing at such foolishness, the emir agreed and wrote a decree permitting Abu Khan to kill any fly. From that day on, no fly was safe from Abu Khan's stick. He hit flies on food, on turbans, on horses – anywhere. And if

In a bowl of china
are mixed two liquids
with colours unmixed.

Egg

63

someone complained, Abu Khan simply showed them his decree and kept on swinging his stick. Soon, everyone was talking about Abu Khan's war on the flies.

One day, Abu Khan went to listen to the emir as he sat judging a difficult case. All at once, Abu Khan jumped up and hit the emir very hard on his back. The emir's guards seized Abu Khan as the emir shouted in pain.

"Sir, I was only hitting a fly," said Abu Khan quickly as he showed the decree. "And you yourself gave me permission."

The emir could do nothing, Abu Khan was right. So as the emir rubbed his back, Abu Khan bowed and left, saying loudly, "The flies deserved their punishment, because they came into my house to take what was not theirs!"

talk about

Sometimes, some rules apply to some people and some other rules apply to other people.

Bangladesh

Bangladesh is a new nation in an ancient land, situated in the plains of the Ganga (Padma) - Brahmaputra delta, one of the world's most fertile plains. A nation hit by too many floods and natural catastrophes, it has, however, pioneered the successful concept of micro-credit to help the poorest sectors. This land of quiet beauty hosts an abundance of bird life as well as the Royal Bengal tiger of the Sundarban mangrove forests, which also shelter the Indian bear, seven species of deer, and the leopard. The population is ethnically homogeneous, the official language is Bangla, and the majority of people are Muslim. Bangla culture, shared historically with neighbouring West Bengal in India, boasts a long literary tradition with icons Rabindranath Tagore and Kazi Nazrul Islam. The powerful music of the Bauls there (a subsect of Sufism) conveys strong messages of love and compassion, as does the story that follows.

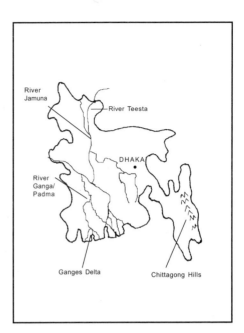

The Making of a Musician

IT WAS A TIME OF TERROR, a time when bandits roamed freely in sixteenth century Bangladesh. Innocent travellers frequently lost their gold and sometimes their lives. No road seemed safe. And in these desperate times, people especially feared a thief named Kenaram.

Kenaram suffered as a child: his mother died soon after his birth, and his father left for a pilgrimage, never to return. His uncle watched him until Kenaram was three, when a terrible famine caused great havoc. The uncle was forced to sell Kenaram to a robber, whose sons all led different gangs. Raised in a violent atmosphere, Kenaram grew into a skilled killer and thief. His name quickly became one of the most notorious in the land.

Now one day, the saintly Bangshi Das walked with his disciples through the forests where Kenaram often roamed. As they journeyed, they sang and praised the goddess Manasa Devi, for Bangshi Das was her devotee as well as a skilled poet-singer. Suddenly, Kenaram and his men appeared in front of them, loudly demanding their gold.

"You may gladly take all that we own. But we have only torn clothing and old rice," replied Bangshi Das. "It is sad indeed that you commit crimes for earthly wealth which will soon vanish yet don't care for the real treasure — devotion to the goddess."

Kenaram was surprised to find someone talking so calmly and bravely to him. Most people only shivered and closed their eyes in fear. He asked the man, "Who are you to talk so boldly to me, the famous and feared Kenaram?"

"I am called Bangshi Das," the singer said simply.

"The one whose songs are said to melt even a stone?"

"Yes, but though they might melt a stone, they may not melt the stony heart of a robber."

"No, no song could ever touch me," roared Kenaram with a laugh. "Now throw down what you have for me, then prepare to die."

"We're not afraid to die," answered the poet, "but may we sing one last time to the goddess before we leave this earth?"

Impressed by the man's courage, Kenaram put his sword back into its sheath and said, "As long as my sword stays still, you may sing."

In the soft twilight, the musicians began to sing in voices rich with devotion. They sang a favourite local song of Behula, the young bride, who ventures to the regions of death with her husband's corpse, to revive him. The words were so full of faith, the notes so pure that suddenly Kenaram threw away his sword and began to weep. Again and again, he begged Bangshi Das to keep singing, promising him all of his wealth.

"I do not want your wealth," answered the poet.

"Then I don't want it either," said Kenaram and ordered his men to dig up his riches and throw them in the river. When that was done, Kenaram took his sword and held it to his heart

"If you won't sing your songs for me and help to save me, I will kill myself," he threatened. Now Bangshi Das was convinced of the robber's sincerity. He sang for hours to the thief, then spoke to him at length of faith, of prayer and devotion. Kenaram followed Bangshi Das from that day on, becoming his most faithful disciple. Ashamed of his great crimes, he prayed and sang at all times, trying to remove some of his past sins.

Thus, for many more years, he roamed the forests of Bangladesh, not as a thief but as a singer and devotee. At times, he would even sing to those he had robbed. And the power of his faith was so great, the fire of his song so strong, that even those he had harmed wept tears of joy when they heard his voice.

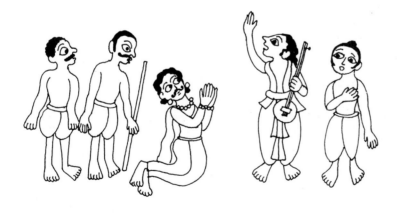

Bhutan

This isolated kingdom is regarded by many as a 'living museum', being one of the most well-preserved, pristine cultures today. Mountains cover the land, except for a small strip of subtropical plains in the south. Known as Drak Yul, 'land of the thunder dragon', Bhutan today is moving toward major democratic reforms under a dynamic king. Although the national language is Dzongkha, Nepali and Sharchop are widely spoken. Every aspect of living is guided by the national religion, Drukpa Kagyu Buddhism. All Bhutanese art, dance, drama and music are steeped in Buddhism. Visual and performing traditions, rich in symbolism, portray the fundamental religious theme of good vs evil. These traditions are celebrated in Bhutan's spectacular religious festival called *Tsechu*. Buddhist tales are also told, as well as stories of the *yeti*, or *migoi*, like this one shared by Kunzang Choden of Bhutan.

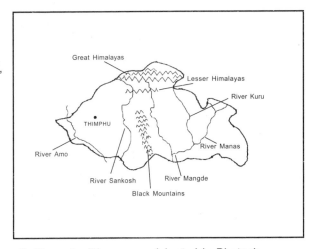

The Ani and the Migoi

DANGBO..O.. DINGBO..O.. past the deep forest, clinging onto the rocks on the side of the mountain, was a cluster of five huts which were occasionally used by meditators as a hermitage. It now happened that one year, an ani or nun was the sole occupant of these huts. She lived in the smallest hut, the one closest to the stream. She had undertaken to do the *losum chosum* meditation of three years of absolute isolation.

The lonely days turned to lonelier months, but after the first nine months of sheer loneliness she suddenly began to experience blissful tranquillity. She then no longer felt the pangs of hunger that so tormented her in the initial days. She ate a little flour and drank some butterless tea once a day more as a daily ritual than as a means to quench her hunger and her thirst. Her mind was at peace and she radiated peace and tranquillity.

It was her third winter by herself. She was no longer afraid of anything for she had overcome every kind of fear. So it was a sense of curiosity that was stirred when she heard a tremendous sound of heavy thumping and shuffling. The sound was accompanied by a very strong smell that nearly choked her. She waited in quiet anticipation as the sound drew closer to her hut and the smell became stronger.

All at once, a heavy shadow fell across the room and then suddenly there was an enormous effort of something being pushed through the window. The little room in which she sat became dark as the window was filled with the bulk of some strange creature's leg. The little hut actually shook under its weight. It was a leg that looked like no other leg. It was something between a human leg and an animal leg. It was about two times the size of a yak leg and covered with fur. The fur was of a dark colour but because of the darkness the exact colour was difficult to tell.

It was with serene composure that the ani wondered what she should do. Then as her eyes adjusted to the partial

67

darkness she saw that a large bamboo stake had pierced the foot right through and was still stuck there. There was some blood and pus in the fur around the piece of bamboo. She saw that the creature was in need of help and this was its way of seeking it.

The ani took her penknife and then tried to extract the bamboo. After a long period of labour, covered in perspiration and dizzy from the foul smell of the creature, she was finally able to get the stake out. It was about a foot long. She then took some sanctified butter and applied it lavishly to the wound.

After a while, the strange leg was withdrawn through the window with as much effort as when it was pushed in. Slowly the great mass of the creature moved away with a heavy thumping and crashing noise. With the fading noise, the strong smell died away too. The ani felt a shudder down her spine as she wondered aloud, "Perhaps that was a migoi."

From then on, as if to thank the ani, the strange creature kept coming back to the hut bringing with it different kinds of game. The carcasses of deer, wild boar, birds, and other animals were regularly shoved through the window. It is said that the ani was greatly disturbed by these occurrences. Her meditation was senseless if this creature was to continue to take the lives of other creatures for her sake. So she had to move away to another hermitage to complete her meditation.

talk about

What do you do when scary thoughts will not go away?

India

With the Himalayas to the north and a coastline along the Bay of Bengal, the Indian Ocean and the Arabian Sea, irrigated by several rivers, including the mighty Ganga and Brahmaputra, and the Indo-Gangetic plain and Deccan Plateau in between, India is a land of diversity. From the lions of the Gir forest in the west to the mass nesting of the olive ridley sea turtles on the east coast, the country supports a variety of flora and fauna which, however, cry to be protected with greater vigilance. It has a population second only to China, a myriad official and unofficial languages, and a variety of cultures and ways of life. India has been a democracy since it became independent in 1947. It is known for beautiful crafts and exquisite weaves, and has a long history of oral storytelling. Regional cuisines, too, are reaching the rest of the world. Although the dominant faith is Hinduism, many Muslims and those from other faiths have lived together for much of India's history. Below are two short tales: about the popular god Ganesh, and a true story to show Indian hospitality.

The Scratch

ONE DAY, little Ganesh was entertaining himself in the garden while his mother, the Goddess Parvati, was inside. Looking for more mischief, he picked up a kitten and played quite roughly with it. As he did this, he scratched the kitten, without knowing. Finally tired of his game, he ran inside and was amazed to see his mother's face bleeding.

"Mother, who did that to you?" he asked, full of fury. "I will teach them a lesson right away."

"But my son, you did it," she replied sadly. "You played roughly with the kitten and hurt her. And if you harm any part of nature, you harm the rest. Everything is connected. So when you scratched the kitten, you scratched me as well. Be careful, my son."

The Visit

ONCE A COUPLE went to visit the city of Ayodhya in North India. With them they carried a letter from their friends, the Rastogi family in Delhi. It was addressed to a brother who lived in Ayodhya, asking him to take good care of the visitors. The couple arrived in the evening after a hot, crowded train ride and debated what to do. The city was new to them and they had only a letter with a name, but no address or phone number. They showed the name on the envelope to several ricksha drivers at the train station.

"I know the family. They live not too far away. Climb in," said an older driver at last. They got into his ricksha and he started pedalling. After many turns and

The red queen who stands between strings of pearls In a red palace.

¡ənɓuoʇ ɹnoʎ

twists down small lanes and large, they arrived at a house, paid the driver, and introduced themselves, presenting the letter.

"Please come in. You must be tired," said the homeowner as his wife brought refreshing tea. Gratefully, the weary couple sipped tea, bathed, then shared a meal of chapati and dal with their new hosts. Feeling very comfortable and well taken care of, they enjoyed a fine sleep.

In the morning after a leisurely breakfast, the man of the house spoke. "Now that you have rested and are feeling stronger, I will take you to the right place."

The two from Delhi looked at each other in surprise as their host continued. "You see, our name is Rastogi, but we have no relatives in Delhi. We do not know your friends there, and we have never heard of their brother here. Last night, though, it was late and you were tired. We did not want to upset you or send you away. We were happy to offer what little we could. Now, this morning, I have made inquiries and found the correct address."

With a smile, he led the very bewildered but thankful couple to the right Rastogi family. There they stayed for several days, and the week ended as nicely as it began, thanks to the unquestioning warmth of Indian hospitality.

A blossoming flower that can't be picked.

The sun.

talk about
When telling a lie is
not really a lie.

70

The Maldives

A republic since 1968, the Maldives, with the smallest population of any Asian nation, lies southwest of Sri Lanka and is composed of about 1200 small coral islands (with almost 200 inhabited). There is little arable land; the islands yield mainly coconut, millet, cassava, yams and tropical fruit, so almost all other principal food items are imported. Main industries are fishing, tourism, shipping, coconut processing and garment manufacturing. The Maldives is almost exclusively Islamic, and Dhivehi is the language spoken. Reed mats stained with natural dyes, and lovely wooden lacquerware are the principal crafts. In a Web article, Hassan Thakuru of the Maldives used a small story from his grandfather to show the problems of too much power in the hands of one man.

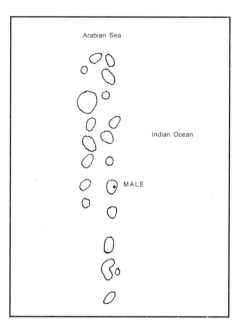

Monkey's Climb

ONCE UPON A TIME, in the land of animals, the monkey used to boast about its ability to climb the tallest tree in the land. He invited other animals to join him so they could look at the beauty of the landscape from above. The Sheep, Monkey's good friend, said he would rather not venture up trees. He preferred to be on the solid ground to see and touch reality.

Some animals tried to join Monkey in tree climbing, but they could not go as high as Monkey could. So they gave up, while warning Monkey of the dangers of going too far high up the trees.

One day, Monkey found the tallest tree. Ignoring the warnings of the other animals, Monkey went on higher and higher — until he felt he could touch the sky. All the animals were under the tree, admiring Monkey as he climbed.

"Stop! It is enough!" they warned him. But he would not listen. When he had climbed to the top of the tree, he celebrated and danced on the branches, shaking all the leaves and flowers up there. But when he looked down, the cows, the goats, the elephants, the lions, all of the animals were dying of laughter.

As Monkey returned to the ground, he asked why they laughed so much. "The higher the monkey climbs, the more it exposes its bottom," Sheep said.

And so it is with power of any kind. The higher one ascends tree of power, the more the public have a chance to observe and scrutinise one's political or economic bottom!

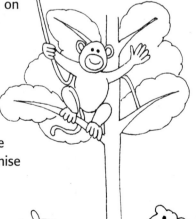

Nepal

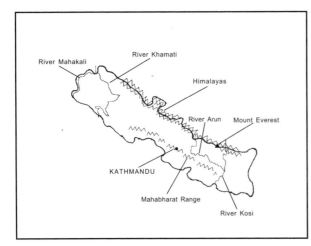

Nepal, a small landlocked country, is a region of extremes: a mere 160 sq km separates the Himalayas to the north – home to yaks, snow leopards, and eight of the world's ten highest peaks – from the humid south with its elephants, rhinoceroses and tigers. Nepal, which has the deepest river gorge in the world, is a melting pot of many races and tribes. Nepali is the national language and written in Devnagari script. Recent years have seen much change, with a move from an unstable monarchy to a new democracy. Agriculture, the dominant occupation, influences many important folk performing arts of Nepal, while the highly symbolic Nepali arts and crafts explore the religious themes of Hinduism and Tantric Buddhism. Traditional crafts include wood-carving, stone sculpture, and religious painting, including vivid images of deities and demons. The clever young woman below uses such imagery to play a fine trick.

Give Us Rice

ONCE IN NEPAL, a mother, father, five sons, and their five wives all lived in a big farmhouse. Each one worked very hard every day, but the mother was a stingy type. Although they had several barns full of good rice, she never let anyone eat it.

Instead, for every meal, she cooked the cheapest food possible – a paste boiled from cornflour. Day after day, the sons and their wives went out to the fields and worked long hours. Night after night, when they returned with great hunger, they were given just this rough food. At last, the five wives grew very angry.

"She has so much rice, but we never taste any," the eldest complained.

"If she won't share," said the youngest and most clever, "then we must take the food ourselves."

"But she'll find out and punish us," warned another wife.

"Don't worry," replied the youngest. "I have a plan."

So the next day, while the mother napped, the wives crawled under the biggest barn. Gently they pushed up a floorboard, crept into the barn, and took some rice. They carried it out to the fields where they husked it, boiled it, and enjoyed each warm, delicious grain. Then, very quietly, they put back the empty rice husks.

The following day, they took some rice to the market, sold it and bought nice vegetables and dal – lentils – to cook with. Week after week, month after month passed with such secret feasting. But at last, all of the rice in the biggest barn had been eaten.

"We must do something soon, or we'll be discovered," the wives whispered to each other, suddenly afraid.

"I know what we can do," said the youngest. She told them her plan and everyone agreed.

Late that night, they crawled out of bed and put on strange make-up and

Honey when you eat it, but cotton when you spit it out.

Sugarcane.

72

old clothes. They now appeared very different and very frightening.

Next, each one picked up a pan or a drum. Suddenly a great noise sounded in the house.

"FEED US, FEED US, WE WANT RICE!" screamed scary voices as drums and banging sounds sounded.

"Husband, wake up," said the mother. "Who is making such a dreadful noise?" The two shivered under the blankets as they heard bodies moving through the house. They peeked out to see fierce monsters dancing wildly. Then again they heard loud and terrible voices crying, "FEED US NOW!"

The two felt too scared to move. They called out, "Take rice, take rice, as much as you like, from the big barn!" More beats and shrieks were heard, then the sounds of loud footsteps going to the barn. At last it was silent, but the parents still couldn't sleep. They hid in their bed until birds welcomed dawn.

Early the next day, when the wives came for tea, the mother asked them, "Did you hear monsters last night?"

The wives tried not to giggle as they answered. A few said they heard something, but were too scared to check. Others said that they slept without hearing a sound. The old couple then went to the biggest barn and found only empty husks – all the rice was gone!

"See, you silly woman," said her husband. "For many years, you were too stingy and never gave anyone a good meal. Now all the rice is gone. We never enjoyed it. Those monsters ate up every grain."

The old woman felt very sorry and sad. "I was wrong," she admitted. "From now on, we'll all enjoy good food and leave nothing for greedy monsters!'

So from that day on, the mother was very generous. She cooked rice, dal and the best of fresh vegetables. The good food gave everybody strength to work harder and harder, so the family became quite wealthy. Thus, everyone lived together in peace and the wives never, ever had to sneak food again.

talk about
The things you can do
on a full stomach.

Pakistan

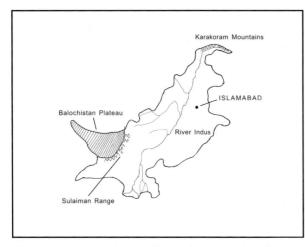

Pakistan, 'land of the pure', is the cradle of the Indus Valley civilisation, dating back 4,500 years. The remains of the advanced ancient cities of Mohenjodaro and Harappa are found there, along with Buddhist temples, Muslim tombs, and ruins from the Mughal times. The Hindu Kush, Karakoram and Himalayan ranges extend into the fertile Indo-Gangetic plains, and the Tharparkar desert in Sindh is the only fertile desert in the world. Today, most of the population is Muslim, the national language is Urdu, and the ethnic composition is made chiefly of Punjabi and Seraiki-speaking people. Traditional crafts include clay pottery, embroidery, block printing, and crafts made from camel skin and hair. Pakistani music includes the semi-classical ghazal, the devotional *qawwali* and modern blends. Stories told include those of Sufi saints, heroes past and present, and clever women.

The Generous Wife

It flew away without feathers and wings, with only a thread tied to its neck.

A kite.

IN BEAUTIFUL PAKISTAN, a man often stood outside the masjid and said, "Give of your goods to charity, give to the masjid. Whoever shall give to the masjid, the same shall have *houris* in heaven."

One day, his wife went near the masjid and heard his words. She felt inspired to give freely and made a vow to share more of her goods. She hurried home, prepared delicious food, then sent it to him. Not knowing the source, he smiled rather greedily when he saw the feast.

"Some excellent person gives fine food. He shall be blessed with houris and have a great reward in heaven," he shouted to all who passed by. "Do all of you as he did and give, give, give." He devoured the food all day and returned home unable to eat even one little bean.

"I ate too much rich food today, given by a most charitable believer," he explained to his wife.

"I am glad you enjoyed it," said his wife. "Because all the nice food was sent by me."

"What?" he cried. "YOU sent it?"

"Yes certainly," she said happily. "I heard you urge everyone to give and I made a vow to share more of our goods, just as you said."

"Oh, I shall die," said the man. "You foolish woman, how can you give away our goods?"

"I only did what you suggested," she said.

"My words are for other people — for those foolish enough to give away wealth. They are not meant for you to destroy this house." Then he stretched himself out on the cot and said, "I think I will die."

"Whether you die or not," said his wife, "I have made a vow to give and I will." Soon, some neighbours came in, saw the husband silent on the cot, and

74

cried, "What is wrong?"

"Alas," cried the wife, "he is not breathing anymore." So they began to lay him out. When they went to get supplies for burial, his wife whispered to him, "Why do all this? Even if you go, your goods will be given away for funeral expenses."

"Spend no money on me," he said. "Simply lay a shroud over my body. But if you promise not to waste any more of my goods, I'll get up and live."

"No, no, I have made the vow and it must be kept," insisted his wife. So the shroud was put over the body. Then she told people to move outside, so she could have a moment alone with her departed husband. She bent over and whispered again, "Don't be foolish. They will soon carry you to the grave. Get up."

"I will consent to live, if you promise to stop giving our money away so foolishly," he whispered back.

"I have made a vow and it must be kept," said she, shaking her head. Then she called to those waiting outside. Gently, they carried him and placed him in a shallow grave. Finally, someone said the prayers. The wife asked for one last look at her husband. She stepped down to him and whispered, "In minutes, loads of earth will be thrown on you. Stand up and come home."

"Will you promise to stop giving?" he asked.

"I have promised and so I must give," she said firmly.

"Then let them cover me up. The sooner, the better," he cried. She stepped out and said, "Shovel in the earth."

As soon as a little dirt was thrown, she cried, "Hear me now, since my husband is dead, the whole of his house and goods I give to the poor." Hearing those words, the man was truly shocked.

"Before it was only a little she vowed in charity," he thought. "Now my whole house is being wasted." Instantly he sprang to his feet and, leaping from the grave, he dropped his shroud and raced back to take possession of his house.

As he fled naked, the people were astonished and cried, "Ah this man must be a great saint for he's come back from the dead."

So they all chased after him, with cries of praise, while his wife returned home with a grin to prepare another donation.

Sri Lanka

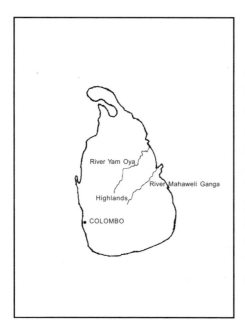

Sri Lanka, located to the southeast of India and long a centre of Buddhism, has a human history dating back to the Paleolithic age. The Sinhalese are in the majority with Tamils forming the largest ethnic minority. Sinhala and Tamil are the two official languages. The pear-shaped island has plains rising to mountains in the south-central regions. Famous for its tea, coffee, rubber and coconuts, Sri Lanka boasts a progressive and modern industrial economy. Traditions of dancing and drumming continue, and the art of mask-making in the low-country tradition as well as the art of puppetry in coastal areas are being preserved by craft guilds there. Proverbs are often shared, some with stories. This story's proverb, 'Like going to get the *laha* made bigger' is said when one's words worsen a problem! The laha is a grain measure, the equivalent of about three-and-a-half kilos.

The Laha

The tender leaf that the elephant does not eat.

Fire

IN OLDEN DAYS, villagers had to give part of their rice harvest each year to the king. Now in a certain village, the villagers began to complain.

"The king's portion of paddy is too large," one man said.

"Just see how large the laha is that he uses," said another.

"How can we change this?" asked a third man. Since no one had an answer, an assembly of the villagers met and debated the problem. Finally, they decided to make a respectful request to the king. They would ask him to send a smaller measuring vessel so that his share would be smaller and they would be able to survive. One man was chosen to go to the ruler and explain the situation.

He set forth bravely enough, carefully practising his words. But the closer he got to the palace, the less brave he felt. As he went through the palace gates, his knees started to shake. When, at last, he was ushered into the king's presence, he was sick with fear.

"Why have you come?" asked the king, somewhat sternly.

The poor villager, quaking all over, forgot everything he had rehearsed. He whispered in fright, "I came, Your Majesty, to get the laha made bigger." Of course, this was exactly the opposite of what the village wanted, but the man was just too scared to say the right words.

The king, however, was delighted and quickly agreed. He at once ordered that the contribution from the man's village would be increased from then on, since they wanted the laha made bigger.

When the man returned home with the sad news, the other villagers quickly decided that they should simply have kept their mouths shut. But it was too late. And now those poor villagers are remembered only through this proverb. So when you hear "Like going to get the laha made bigger," then you, too, will remember when to talk and when not to!

VISUAL ARTS

ARTS OF WAR

The beautiful carpets made in Afghanistan have had a new look in recent years.
Now, in addition to the typical geometric and floral designs, tanks, guns, or other scenes of war are also found. Often the 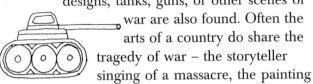 arts of a country do share the tragedy of war – the storyteller singing of a massacre, the painting of a battle, the song of a people's resistance. See if students can adapt an art form to give a message.

Materials

Writing surface and materials

Method

❖ Ask students how war and struggle are reflected in art around the region: cartoons, posters, paintings, sculptures.

❖ Tell them how traditional Afghan carpet weavers have adapted their designs by now weaving tanks and helicopters and other symbols of war into their carpets.

❖ As a class, choose one struggle – in your nation, the region, or the world. Brainstorm ways that the tragedy could be shown in art projects to help others stop the war and work for peace. Art projects can be stories/poems told and written, paintings and sculptures made, plays performed, and so much more.

❖ Design the pieces on paper and, if time, materials, and energy allow, some students may wish to actually create their pieces, moving beyond the design stage.

FLOOR DECORATIONS

Beautiful Indian floor decorations (such as *kolam, alpana, rangoli*) welcome the guest in India, with intricate designs and sometimes fine colour covering the doorstep, the area in front of the door and, during festivals, the entire street. These greetings in art share the warm spirit of hospitality found in the story of the Rastogis.

Both boys and girls can enjoy the challenges of floor decoration.

Materials

Ground/floor, white and coloured chalk

Methods

❖ For students new to kolams, introduce the concept of the kolam as a welcoming design. Draw a few on the board or ground, using designs below or ones that you know.

❖ If students know about kolams, invite some to share their favourite designs.

❖ Have students work outside to create new kolams. They can place dots down in grids first, as in some traditions, or simply draw freehand.

❖ Enjoy the colour carpets.

TRUCKS OF PAKISTAN

Although brightly decorated vehicles, like the rickshaws of Bangladesh, are found elsewhere in South Asia, vehicle art in Pakistan is exceptional. Many trucks are covered top to bottom with landscapes, portraits, calligraphic poetry, religious verses, and more. Students can enjoy exploring this idea.

Materials

Ground/slate and chalk or paper and colours
Description below

Method

❖ Ask students if they've seen brightly decorated vehicles in pictures or on streets near them.

❖ Read and note the typical types and placement of decorations on trucks, below.

❖ Have students make a truck outline – on ground, paper, or slate.

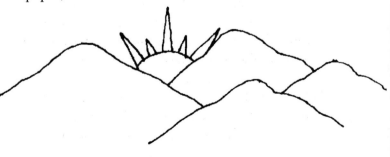

- Using ideas from Pakistan, and adding their own ideas, students decorate their trucks (this can be a nice small group project if the truck is big enough).
- Share the creations.

Source material

Many trucks follow this rough plan for their decorations:

Above the cab usually mosques, the Ka'bah, and other holy monuments.

Side panels waterfalls, lakes, snow-capped mountains, landscapes and animals (e.g. tigers chasing deer) hunting lodges, fighter jets and missiles

Back a single large portrait surrounded by flowers, vines and geometric designs (portrait of hero, film star, athlete or – recently – the truck-owner's son!) Sayings – original, religious, or literary – can be written in various places. One favourite is "If your mother prays for you, it's like a breeze from heaven."

VERBAL/WRITTEN ARTS

THE YETI

Storytellers around the world love to tell about strange and fearful creatures. The yeti of the Himalayan region is one of the more famous 'mystery' monsters. There are many legends of the yeti, and sketchy reports from British explorers, Sherpas, and others of huge footprints or a large 'ape-man'. But to this day, no real evidence exists, unless your students can find him...!

Materials

Pen and paper

Method

- After students read 'The Ani and the Migoi', ask if any have heard or read anything about the yeti. Go over whatever is known, from story or elsewhere. Have them research it on the Internet, if available.
- When students have enough background info, ask them to be explorers or villagers high up in the Himalayas. Then, one day as they

venture further up the mountain than usual, they, too, catch a glimpse of the yeti or his footprint.
- Have them write an excited letter home describing how they made their discovery and what they now believe about the yeti!

TRUE STORY

True stories from our lives are so important to share. I love the simple true story from my dear friend, Dr Rastogi, because it shows how deep Indian hospitality is. But all kinds of true stories are important for students to tell. Even if they don't share a specific value, they share a part of being human.

Materials

List of beginning family story themes below, written on board

Method

- After students read Dr Rastogi's story (and other true stories in the book), talk about the importance of sharing family true stories. Find out when and how students share their true stories with friends and families – in the playground, on the bus, at bedtimes?
- Have children look at the list on the board and think of one simple, short true story that happened to them, or any of their family/friends.
- Students should then practise it quietly – saying the story then sharing it with a partner.
- After partner work, small groups can form, with each student sharing her/his story.
- Some students can share with the whole class. And when these examples are finished, find other ways to keep true stories told often in your classroom.

Source Material: religious events, tricks, animals, strange events, tales of lying, fools, heroes, friendship, festivals, chance and fate, nature, accidents, toys/games, sports, fights, first times, being lost, trips, special times, getting in trouble, wise ones, lost fortunes, name stories, family lore, injustices, challenges, victories, embarrassing moments.

 SONGS/GAMES

 NATURE/SCIENCE

A RHYME

This little Bangla rhyme from Bangladesh plays with rhymes, rhythms, and nonsense words to paint a humorous picture of a devoted son-in-law in a society that values family greatly.

Materials and Method

Share the words below as best you can (sound hint: ai as in eye, a as in ah, i as ee, om as ome). Have students learn the rhyme, and say it in the steady rhythms of a train.

> Aaikom baaikom taaraataari
> Jodu Maashtaar shoshoor baari
> Rail kompo jhomaajhom
> Jodu Maashtaar aaloor dom.

> Aikom baikom Jodu Master (teacher)
> Runs to in-law's in a haste,
> Rail journey full of jerking
> Made Jodu like potato paste.

RAIN SONG

From my friend, Shanta Gangoli, comes this little chant in Marathi, one of India's many languages.

Materials and Method

Write or read the song in the phonetic pronunciation. Show the actions, matching numbers. Have students sing with you, while doing actions.

Ye-reh ye-reh paavsa	Come, come, rain
Tula dayto pie-saa	I'll give you money
Pie-sa zaala khotaa	The money is fake
Pavoos aalaa mohtaa	The rain comes down.

Actions

1. Look up to sky, use both hands, palms up, to call rain.
2. Right hand pretends to pick money from left open palm and offer it up to rain.
3. Look very sadly at empty palms, then turn hands over to show they're empty.
4. Both hands keep waving downward to mime a heavy rain.

THE ART OF THE GARDEN

The Islamic world holds gardens in high regard – as pieces of paradise. Students can consider the uses of gardens as they plan one.

Materials

All types of natural materials in your environment: flower petals, pebbles, shells, twigs, sand, etc. Quotation below

Method

- ❖ Read the quotation below.
- ❖ Discuss some of the gardens that students may have seen, in books or in person. Explore how a garden is designed.
- ❖ Consider how gardens vary from region to region, due to materials available and cultural ideas.
- ❖ Working in small groups, outside, students now design a small garden. Each uses whatever natural materials they can, and works in a small area, probably less than one square metre. Water should also be a part of it in some way, for this was very important.
- ❖ When finished, take a walk through your lovely garden displays.

Source Material: In all Muslim languages, the word *jannat* (garden) means heaven. For the eye, there is the green of the plants, the beauty of the rivers. For the ear, there is the music of the birds, the music of the waterfalls. For the smell, there is the perfume of the flowers. For the taste and touch, there are the fruits. (Mantin: 1993, 47)

A BIG WEB

When little Ganesh scratches his mother, he finds out how connected everything is. Students can reinforce their understanding of the web of life after reading the story.

Materials

Large papers and colours

Method

- After the story is read, read the words of a Mongolian writer below, who shares a very wide image of the web of nature. Ask students to share ways in which parts of nature are connected in a small area: in their own regions or in desert, city, seashore, forest, etc.
- Have students work in small groups, each with one large paper. Challenge each group to decide what small area of nature they will illustrate.
- Ask students to draw a web to show connections in their area (showing which animals support others by providing food or hunting, which plants provide food or oxygen, etc.).
- Encourage them also to show the role of humans in their web, and to state if problems can be caused or helped in the web by human actions, intentional or not.

Source Material: The motion of the atmosphere, sun, moon and stars, the colour of the ground, fitness of cattle, autumn migration of birds, beginning of marmot hibernation – all these are hidden threads connecting nature and human beings. We all are the children of nature. Is it not the real challenge for humans to learn and understand the true meaning of all these connections? (From Mongolia Online www.mongoliatoday.com/issue/7/tales.html)

 THINGS TO THINK ABOUT

FAMILY CHALLENGES

Very often, especially in extended families, there can be differences of opinion between mothers-in-law and daughters-in-law. In 'We Want Rice', the mother-in-law is taught a lesson through a clever trick. Students can think about this problem and consider similar solutions.

Materials

Song below

Method

- After students read 'We Want Rice', read the Oriya song (from India) below to them. Ask if they've heard other songs, proverbs, stories, etc. about these roles. Discuss what else they've heard or read about this challenging family relationship.
- List five or six possible problems, giving concrete situations (e.g. the mother-in-law makes cruel remarks to the daughter-in-law, forbids her to go to a friend's house, ridicules her for not bringing more dowry, etc.)
- Divide class into small groups and have each group choose one problem. Students should then act out the problem, then act out a possible solution or alternative.
- Finish with each group sharing their mini-drama.

Source material

The date palm makes a pleasing sound,
In the father's house the daughter is happy,
But in her mother-in-law's house,
She is just like an oil-pressing machine.

LIKE MOSQUITOES

The Afghan story of Abu Khan relates a fine trick played against a rich and powerful ruler. It is an endless struggle and students need to think clearly about these issues so that, later, they can stand up for the rights of the underdogs.

Materials

Pencil and paper

Methods

- After students have read 'The Flies', discuss the issues raised by the story.
- Next, think about the way that newspaper words can shape opinion and how different papers – some conservative, some liberal, some favouring the upper class, some not – will have different viewpoints and how the same story can be described in very different ways.
- Ask students, in pairs, to write two brief articles describing Abu Khan's situation and solution. They don't need to include every action, just the main points.
- But ask that one article should be written as if by a reporter sympathetic to Abu Khan, while the other one should favour the Emir and make Abu Khan look wrong.
- Post the various articles on the board for students to compare and discuss.

Stories and Activities
Southeast Asia

THE REGION

SOUTHEAST ASIA OFFERS A VIBRANT MIX of cultures, religions, and languages, with a rich heritage. Since most of the region is in the tropical belt, the climate remains quite constantly hot, although hills and mountains in some areas provide cool breezes as well. Sugar palm trees, rubber trees, rice, coconut, mangoes, durians, and many other plants thrive here. The great Mekong River winds through the heart of Southeast Asia, offering its riches and its stories. Rain forests are found as well in the region, although they are being cleared at an alarming rate. Fortunately, some – like the famed Taman Negara of Malaysia – are saved as national parks while others, like Batu Apoi in Brunei, are studied for their incredible diversity of plant and animal life.

Long coastlines and a wealth of islands helped maritime empires to develop here. As trade grew, kingdoms did too. Malay sultans fought with each other and inland empires blossomed in Thailand, Burma, and Cambodia. In Cambodia's city of temples, Angkor, one sees the early influence of Hinduism, which later gave way to Buddhism in much of the region, while Islam became dominant in Brunei, Indonesia, and Malaysia. Chinese influence was felt strongly in Vietnam, which they controlled for 1000 years. But the promise of wealth in this diverse region brought armed boats from Western Europe as well. From the first days of the Portuguese, through the Dutch, the English, and the French, the region has suffered greatly from imperialism. Thailand, however, remained independent throughout this colonial period.

During World War II, the Japanese invaded and ruled harshly from Burma to Indonesia, finally leaving at the end of the war. Independence movements sprouted: the most famous being that of Ho Chi Minh in Vietnam. The Dutch, after great struggle, left Indonesia, while the U.S. left the Philippines more quietly. The British slowly turned over their colonies as well. For most of the region, independence had finally arrived. However, after independence from France came to Laos, Cambodia, and Vietnam in the mid twentieth century, the Americans pushed into the region during the Vietnam War, causing a disastrous loss of life and land.

The years since then have been full, as economic development moved much of the region forward. Democratic as well as socialist governments, the military dictatorship in Myanmar and others co-exist across the area. Education is widespread throughout the region, literacy rates are fairly high, and the position of women is relatively good. The Islam of Southeast Asia is more moderate than some forms in West Asia, and the role of Muslim women today reflects the stronger status they've had historically in the region. Today, the region boasts great contrasts: high tech energy and ancient remains, rain forests and skyscrapers, shadow puppets and Thai boxing. The future indeed holds promise for this varied region, and its stories have much to share.

. . . and its STORIES

Years ago, storyteller Prof. Wajuppa Tossa of northeastern Thailand found her beloved Isan culture threatened by the stronger Thai language and culture, so she began work to cultivate storytelling in the Isan language. She now teaches storytelling to her students, sends them out in troupes to share their Isan heritage, translates old Isan epics, and runs yearly storytelling summer camps.

In Singapore, the National Library Board and its storytelling librarians, and the National Book Development Council under the vision of R. Ramachandran, are helping Singaporeans explore both cultural storytelling roots and future directions. The Asian Storytelling Network, formed in 2001 by popular tellers Sheila Wee and Kiran Shah, seeks to "revive the oral tradition of storytelling in Singapore" while creating an appreciation for Asian folktales.

Nearby, in Malaysia, traditional tellers have different styles, but none of them are thriving now. In Kelantan, the storytelling form of the blind *awang selampit* or *tok selampit* features long tales of kings and spirits sung to the accompaniment of a two-stringed fiddle. In Perlis, in northwestern Malaysia, the storyteller in the awang batil form chants his romances to a tune while drumming his fingers on a bowl or pot. The most professional are the tukang cerita, professional storytellers, who tell long, well-embellished romances. (Osman: 1999, 140)

Recently, efforts have been made to introduce storytelling in schools, and an Asian Storytellers' Conference was sponsored some years ago by the National Library. The lively children's bookstore, Trisha & Sasha's, in Kuala Lumpur, and the busy children's library started by teller Judy Shaik have, for years, also sponsored storytelling programmes for children, parents, and teachers.

Meanwhile, indigenous people in the Islamic nation of Brunei Darussalam are experiencing a storytelling problem felt throughout Asia: the challenge of attracting listeners to older forms of storytelling. Eva Maria Kershaw, who recently collected Dusun language folk tales in Brunei, writes that "the narration of folktales in Dusun villages was abandoned around 1975, hastened by the arrival of battery-powered television sets in even the remotest areas, but largely owing to the flight of young Dusuns to the townships in search of education and work...(in addition, most of the younger generation) no longer enjoy the storyteller's tales, finding them unsophisticated if not 'offensive' while the bulk of the present-day Dusun children no longer speak

Dusun in any form". (Kershaw: 1999, 122)

In East Java, Indonesia, a relatively informal style of storytelling, *kentrung*, skilfully blends ancient myths and folktales with local history and is shared during certain times. The form's name comes from the sound, 'trung trung', of the tambourine played by the teller. Smaller and larger tambourines also add to the drama, especially in the battle scenes where a vigorous beat heightens the tension. During a woman's seventh month of pregnancy, stories of local legends are told so that the baby in the womb acquires the virtues of the prophets described. Later, right after childbirth, another set of stories is shared, including those of the popular folk hero, Joko Tingkir, which show that even a simple peasant boy, through will and discipline, can reach a high position.

Another form of telling in Indonesia is the *kaba* of the Minangkabau people in Sumatra. In this form, the teller, *tukang kaba*, is accompanied by a flute and a fiddle-like instrument, the *rabab*. He sits on the ground, with the audience surrounding him, and performs the whole night, usually at a life-cycle ceremony, such as childbirth, puberty, marriage. The kaba can instruct as it entertains – educating listeners about local customs and Islamic teaching – and also be a form of social protest. The style can be humorous and poignant, and the words are poetic. Today, the kaba can also be found on tapes and CDs.

In a part of coastal Sumatra is another form using rabab – *rabab pasisia* – which is popular at weddings and even at markets since it features newer stories about modern life.

Dr Murti Bunanta of Indonesia, a children's literature specialist and writer, feels that "storytelling is one of the best ways to instill a love of reading" and so promotes storytelling in that country in various ways, with the support of the Society for the Advancement of Children's Literature (SACL). An annual Storytelling Festival during Children's Day in July has been held for more than 15 years now with artists, diplomats, ministers, educators and others joining in; popular storytelling competitions and workshops for teachers encourage more telling as well.

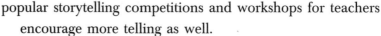

Brunei

The Sultanate of Brunei Darussalam, meaning 'abode of peace', is located on the island of Borneo. Although it has experienced civil strife, colonisation by Europeans, and piracy, it is still considered one of the richest countries in the world due to its extensive petroleum and natural gas fields. Brunei was a monarchy until 2003 when it became a democratic republic. About a third of the population is Malay and Islam is the official religion. The culture is predominantly Malay, but is seen as more conservative than Malaysia. Crafts in Brunei include woven baskets, silver and brassware, while cloth weaving is one of the country's oldest cottage industries. The *Jong Sarat* is the most famous of the various designs, considered a trademark of traditional weaving techniques in Brunei. The short, sweet tale below, of cats, not cloth, was adapted from the stories of the minority Dusan people, collected by Eva Maria Kershaw in the 1980s.

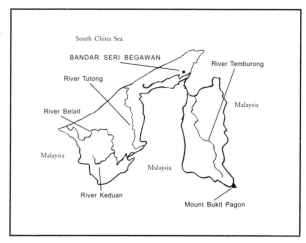

A Widow's True Friends

ONCE A LONELY COUPLE, with no children, decided to tame some cats, to keep them company. Things went very well for a while, until one day the husband grew ill. His wife tried to nurse him, but it was no use. Soon, he breathed his last. So the woman told the cats, "Stay here and I'll call the others."

But as soon as she left the house, the cats quickly turned into human beings, to help their friend. Some went to get firewood, some went to fetch water, some started to cook. They worked quickly, and soon finished the cooking, then spread out the food. Thus it was ready for the guests to eat, as was the custom. Then, at once, they turned back into cats. When the guests arrived, they just saw some lazy cats, sitting and carefully licking themselves clean.

Later, when the rituals were done and the husband was buried, the widow began her period of mourning. Since she seemed lonely at that time, the cats again turned into human beings, to keep her company. Fourteen days passed at last, and her mourning time was over. Just before the villagers returned to see the widow, the cats quickly changed back into animals. So when the guests arrived, they just saw some lazy cats, sitting and carefully licking themselves clean. And never again did the cats change back into humans. But to this day, we still keep cats as our special friends.

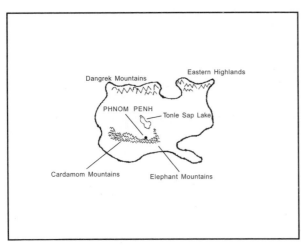

Cambodia

Cambodia's treasures include the Mekong River, the Tonle Sap lake, the temples of Angkor, and the accomplishments of Khmer kings who built rest stops, hospitals and temples. Yet centuries after the great Khmer empires came years of social, cultural and economic oppression from frequent invasions by neighbouring countries and powerful first world nations. The homogeneous population, mostly of Khmer descent, speak Khmer and follow Theravada Buddhism. India's influence is seen especially in the arts: Hindu mythology is carved in stone, and the epic *Ramayana* (*Reamker*) is a source for dance/drama. The elegant court dance tradition is now being revived, along with the country's economy – thanks to tourism and the garment industry – after years of pain and destruction. One Cambodian refugee, Ly Sieng, spoke of her desperate efforts to escape the horrors of those years. Her words are written just as she told them, since although Ly was not yet fluent in English, she was very clear and powerful with her own words.

Ly Sieng's Journey

THE SITUATION WAS SO BAD. Starving, I felt that I shouldn't just sit there and starve to death. You could see so many people dead and starving to death and sick with no medicine and you know that it will come, sooner or later, to you. A few months after my father felt better, I decided to leave.

I planned a trip with a lady and left without telling my father, because I knew he won't let me go. I wrote a letter for my father, telling him that I asked his forgiveness, that the chances of survival were very little. So I left, but we did not make it too far, we were caught. Soldiers stopped us, they searched us, and took everything from me and that lady and put us in prison.

That prison had somewhere between 100 and 200 people – Chinese, Cambodian, young, old, middle-aged. Those people, just like me, were trying to escape and were caught. So they forced all of the people to work from three in the morning until nine or ten in the evening. When anyone escaped and was caught, they killed them in awful ways, to warn us, to scare us.

In seeing all this happen, I think that I have to leave this group, I'm afraid I can't last too long. They put all people in one house, squeezed together. Very hard to sleep, no place to go to the bathroom. We couldn't shower. It was not a life. How could you believe that people would live? I talked to my Cambodian friend; she was too afraid to go. But I knew I had to escape.

So the third day in the evening, I asked the guard for permission to go outside to the bathroom. He let me. Right in front of that building was a big ditch. About three yards wide and deep enough so if someone went inside you could not see the top. Right after I left the building,

I jumped into that ditch. There was water up to my calves. I just ran and ran in that ditch for miles. I heard them screaming for me. I saw lights searching for me, but I just kept going, kept running, kept going.

I ran all night and next day I walked to my village. It was about two in the afternoon. I could not keep going. I was too tired. It was about ten miles (16 km) that I ran. I fell down in the rice field. I took a nap and I made it home at sunset. When my father saw me he was so happy to see me again. My father said you are so lucky that you made it back. I knew I had to try, because if you make it, you make it. If not you die, and that was fine. At that time you didn't care, it just didn't matter anymore. Then my father and I kept working like before.

A couple of months after I came back, my father was too weak to work. But because we did not have enough to eat, on October 1, 1976, he died and they took his body. I don't even know where my father was buried.

talk about

Imagine someone forcibly took away your home. Or you were told you had three days in which to leave the country. Imagine.

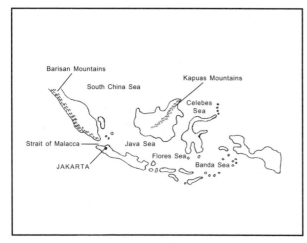

Indonesia

Indonesia, with 17, 508 islands, is the world's largest archipelagic country and the third largest democracy. Trade with India and eastern Asia since the the 4th century enriched the blend of cultures, languages and ethnic groups in Indonesia, home to the world's largest Muslim population. It has a varied ecosystem and is situated on the edge of three continental plates, making it vulnerable to tectonic disturbances. Bahasa Indonesian is the official language, although over 360 languages are spoken there, including the widely spoken Javanese.

Craft traditions include *batik*, *ikat* and *songket* cloth. Indonesia is well known for dances like the elegant *legong*, masked dances/dramas, and shadow puppetry. Performances often feature the rich tones of the *gamelan* orchestra and share Hindu mythology or local legends. Dr Murti Bunanta, who has retold and published many wonderful Indonesian tales, contributed this legend from the province of Papua.

Masarasenani and the Sun

This moving belt can kill you.

It's a snake.

ONCE UPON A TIME there lived a man named Masarasenani. He had a wife and two daughters, Serawiri and Serimini. Every day they went to pound at the sago tree to get its flour. But the yield was barely enough to keep them alive. At that time the day was very short. So before the people finished pounding the sago, night came. Many of the villagers were starving. It continued like this for many, many years. No one knew what to do, until one day Masarasenani had an idea. He planned to meet the Sun, Masarasitumi.

Masarasenani happened to know the place where the sun rose. He noticed that every morning, the sun passed by a narrow rift between two hills. That night, Masarasenani went in secret to that place. Soon he installed a trap. With this trap he intended to catch the sun.

After he was finished, Masarasenani went home. His wife and daughters didn't know about his plan. The following day, as usual, he and his daughters went to pound the sago trees. They worked hard to get as much flour as they could before the sun set. But what happened?

Their sago basket was full, and still the night hadn't come. The villagers were astonished! Why hadn't the sun set? They felt that the day was unusually long. No one knew what was going on except Masarasenani.

Although he was delighted that the villagers could gather more food, he felt restless. He knew that Masarasitumi had been trapped. But he also knew the sun had to be released so that he could do his job and shine on the earth.

Immediately, Masarasenani sent his two daughters home with the sago they had pounded. He was going to release the sun and night would be dark soon. Hurriedly Masarasenani went to the place where the sun had been trapped.

Masarasenani's heart was pounding. Through the trees he spied the trap with Masarasitumi trapped in it. He heard the sun cry, "Masarasenani, please, come quickly. Bring me some *gatal* leaves to cure my leg that is hurt and swollen because

88

of your trap." Now 'gatal' means 'itch' and gatal leaves have always been used to cure itching or swelling in that part of Indonesia.

Masarasenani was surprised that the sun knew who had set the trap. The sun's lamentation touched his heart. He soon appeared from his hiding place, intending to free Masarasitumi.

Seeing Masarasenani coming towards him to help him, the sun said, "Be careful Masarasenani, approach me from the back. Otherwise, you'll be burnt by the rays that pour forth from my face, just like those trees around me." Masarasenani saw that the trees around the sun were all brown and dried up. After the sun had been released, he told Masarasenani the place where he could get gatal leaves to cure his swollen leg. He then also explained the shape of the leaves. Masarasenani left immediately. He soon found the place and took as many leaves as he could carry.

He brought the leaves to the place where the sun was waiting. Masarasenani then helped to rub the leaves onto the sun's swollen legs. Not long after that, the sun's legs were cured.

"Masarasenani, why did you trap me? What have I done wrong?" asked the sun.

"I am sorry, Sun, I had to trap you because my family and all the other villagers were starving. Every day, before we could gather and pound enough sago and other food, you set and the day became dark. And thus we couldn't get enough to eat."

After listening to Masarasenani's complaints, the sun promised to change his behaviour. He agreed to be fair in dividing the time, so that the people had enough time to gather their food and would not starve.

After the sun's legs were completely healed, he went back to the western horizon. Masarasenani went home and told his wife and daughters what had really happened.

From then on, the sun divided day and night equally. He stayed in the sky longer than he did before. So the villagers were very happy because they could gather enough food.

Even today, people call the place where the sun was trapped 'Mayawer', which means 'the trapped sun'. The place where Masarasenani picked the leaves is today a big forest of gatal bushes. And it is said that the gatal leaves of today are not as big as before, when this tale took place. But the people still use them to cure itching and swelling.

talk about
A world without the sun, without fire and light.

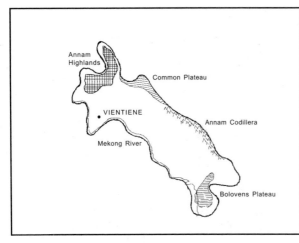

Laos

Laos traces its roots to the Lan Xang dynasty of the 14th century, which included all of present-day Laos and much of Siam. After being occupied by the Thai and the French, it became independent in 1949 and a socialist republic in 1975. Its forested hills and lush, riverfed lowlands are home to the Annamite rabbit, the Saola ox and the Laotian rock rat – all declared living fossils. The population includes a mix of the majority ethnic Lao people and minority Hmong, Yao, Tai Dumm and Dao. Lao is the official language although French, English and minority ethnic languages are also spoken. Harmonies from the popular bamboo mouth organ, the *khaen*, often accompany the favoured *lam* folk singing. Silk and cotton weaving are the most important crafts and Theravada Buddhism deeply influences daily life. The gentle beauty of this land and culture come through in this tale told by Elder Bounyok Saensounthone of Laos, and retold in English by Dr Wajuppa Tossa.

Maeng Nguan, the Singing Cricket

ONE NIGHT, Indra heard a beautiful musical sound that went *"yong, yong, yong"*. He was so pleased that he wanted to give a reward to the singer. He said to his courtiers, "You must bring whoever sang the beautiful song last night, to me. I wish to hear more of the song."

So the courtiers went around making the announcement: "Whoever sang the beautiful song last night must come forward; Great Indra wishes to hear more of your song."

The gecko stepped forward and said, "It's me that sang the beautiful song last night."

"Then tell me what I need to prepare for your performance tonight for Great Indra," said one of the courtiers.

"Oh, you must prepare a good size bamboo pipe and hang it on a pillar in Great Indra's hall," said the gecko.

All was done before night fell. When night fell, the gecko crawled inside the bamboo pipe and began his song, *"thod, thod, thod, tappo, tappo, tappo"*.

Great Indra then said, "Oh, you sang a beautiful song; I will give you a colourful jacket to wear."

In the evening, Great Indra again heard, *"yong, yong, yong"*, the beautiful song. "The song I heard last night was beautiful, but it is not the same," he thought. So, he said to his courtiers, "Do you know that I still hear the beautiful song? The one I heard before the gecko came to sing? Please go and find the singer for me."

The courtiers went out making the same announcement: "Whoever sang a beautiful song last night must come forward; Great Indra wishes to hear more of your song."

.The bullfrog stepped forward and said, "It's me that sang the beautiful song last night."

"Then tell me what I need to prepare for your performance tonight for Great Indra," said one of the courtiers.

"Oh, you must prepare a good size bowl of water and place it at the foot of the stairs of Great Indra's hall," said the bullfrog.

All was done before night fell. When night fell, the bullfrog crawled into the bowl of water and began his song, *"hueng aang, hueng aang, hueng aang".*

Great Indra then said, "Oh, you sang a beautiful song; I will give you a vest to wear."

In the evening, Great Indra again heard, *"yong, yong, yong"*, the beautiful song again. "The song I heard last night was beautiful, but it is not the same," he thought. So, he said to his courtiers, "Do you know that I still hear the beautiful song? The one I heard before the gecko came to sing? Please find the singer for me."

This time the courtiers came across Maeng Nguan, the singing cricket. So they asked, "Did you sing a beautiful song last night?"

"Yes, I did. Why do you ask?" asked Maeng Nguan, the singing cricket.

"Oh, Great Indra wants to hear you sing again tonight. Will you come?"

"Yes, I will come," said Maeng Nguan, the singing cricket.

"Then tell me what I need to prepare for your performance tonight for Great Indra," said one of the courtiers.

"Oh, absolutely nothing. I will just fly and alight on a pillar in Great Indra's hall and sing," said Maeng Nguan, the singing cricket.

That night Maeng Nguan, the singing cricket went to alight on a pillar in Great Indra's hall and began singing, *"yong, yong, yong".*

When Indra heard the song, he felt so delighted that he came out of his hall. "Who sang that heavenly song?" he asked.

"Oh, it is me, Maeng Nguang, the singing cricket, my lord," Maeng Nguan said humbly.

"Then, I will give you gifts," said Indra. "From now, you will be able to see both day and night. And you don't have to eat any ordinary food. You may enjoy heavenly food, dewdrops from heaven."

"Thank you, my lord," said Maeng Nguan. Since then Maeng Nguan, the singing cricket could see both day and night and enjoy heavenly food, dewdrops from heaven. And he continued singing his song: *"yong, yong, yong, yong, yong, yong, yong, yong!"*

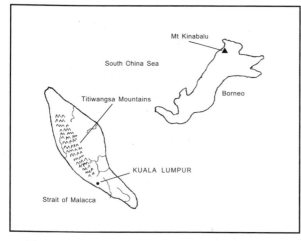

Malaysia

For centuries, various cultures have been drawn to Malaysia by its central location in maritime trade routes among China, India and the Middle East. It attracted colonial powers, too: the Portuguese, the British and the Japanese. Now, a free Malaysia has two regions divided by the South China Sea – Peninsular Malaysia and East Malaysia. Rainforests, long coastlines, and cooler highlands form the physical backdrop for a vital mix of Malay, Chinese, and Indian cultures. Islam is the dominant religion and Malaysia's varied arts include calligraphy, batik, the famed Malay kites, and large spinning tops. *Gendang* drumming and instruments such as the rabab, *seruna*, flutes and trumpets are key elements in musical performances. Stories are told in homes, schools, and in libraries. The two tales below, contributed by librarian Mohd Taib Bin Mohamed, share a popular Malay trickster, Si Luncai, and a legend of the land. (The Malay refrain in 'Si Luncai' means "let it be, let it be".)

Si Luncai

ONE DAY, Si Luncai was found guilty of wrongdoing by the king himself. The king ordered him to be punished, to be thrown into the open sea. So he was placed in a gunny sack and taken by sampan boat to the sea by the royal guards.

While the boat moved, Si Luncai looked out through the gunny sack. He saw some pumpkins in the sampan. Knowing that the guards were tired, Si Luncai offered them a song to give them strength.

"We will soon reach the place where you will be thrown," said a guard. "So do be quiet now."

But Si Luncai was not quiet. He started singing by himself, *"Si Luncai dives with his pumpkin... biarkan, biarkan."* Hearing the lively song, the royal guards soon joined in, singing *"Si Luncai dives with his pumpkin... biarkan, biarkan."* They repeated the song, enjoying themselves and forgetting their mission.

While the guards kept singing loudly, Si Luncai sneaked out of the gunny sack and placed some pumpkins in it instead. Then he quietly grabbed two pumpkins and made his way to the water as the royal guards repeatedly enjoyed the song.

Then when they found the right place, the royal guards threw the gunny sack into the waves and turned back home, sure that Si Luncai was in the sack, positive that he was dead. Nobody saw Si Luncai swim safely to the shore, holding on to the pumpkins. And perhaps he is still there, still singing safely, with a big smile, *"biarkan, biarkan".*

Batu Gajah

SANG KELEMBAI WAS SADDENED because his son died. In order to ease his misery, he strolled along a riverbank. In the river, there were three elephants who liked to tease other animals. Nearby, there was a young man who liked to be alone, and who didn't like those who teased others. Sang Kelembai soon met the three elephants.

"You should not be sad. It was your son who died and not you. You should be grateful to be alive," teased one of the elephants, while the others laughed.

Those words only hurt Sang Kelembai, but he replied, "It is a lucky thing that I have vowed not to swear a curse on anyone. If not . . ."

"If not, what curse would you swear, Sang Kelembai?" asked the elephants.

He replied, "That the three of you should be turned into stone."

Suddenly, the three elephants turned into stone. In the distance, the young man still stood alone, watching. And that place, in the river Sungai Kinta, is known to this day by the name Batu Gajah or Elephant Stone. And many who see the rock, know the story, and remember not to tease, and to talk with kindness instead.

Myanmar

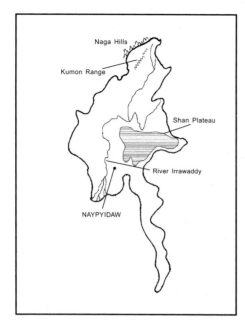

Pagodas greet visitors to Myanmar, for most people today still follow Theravada Buddhism. The majority of the population lives in the fertile river valley of the Irrawaddy, Myanmar's longest river (2170 km). In the 19th century, Britain made Burma part of its Indian Empire, then granted independence in 1948, but today's strict military regime rules a country facing economic challenges. Although the official language is Burmese, Karen and Shan are also spoken. The rubies, sapphires, and jades of Myanmar are famous, as are its paper and wooden toys, cane ware and puppets. Burmese instruments include brass-gong circles, bamboo xylophones, drum circles, and the lovely, decorated boat-shaped string instrument – the *saung gauk*. A most inspiring Burmese woman, Nobel Peace Prize recipient Aung San Suu Kyi, has long worked for political change. Another inspiring woman from older legends is Princess Learned-in-the-Law, whose tales were used for legal study.

Princess Learned-in-the-Law

A box with seven holes.

Your head!

LONG AGO IN OLD BURMA, there lived a king who had to eat fried fish with every meal. One day, however, a terrible storm came. The winds whipped the waves and small boats were broken like straws. No one could go out in the storm to catch fish. So the king did not eat breakfast, for there was no fried fish.

All day, the winds blew and blew. The waves, like wild horses, refused to be tamed and stayed so high that no boat would venture out. So the king did not eat lunch, for there was no fried fish.

As the day passed, the storm still did not die. The king was very hungry by now and quite desperate. He called to his minister.

"Send word out at once," he ordered, "that the fisherman who brings me even one fish for my dinner will have whatever he wishes for a reward." The king's drummers soon carried the message throughout the villages along the coast. Yet even the promise of such a reward was not enough for most fishermen, who feared the roaring sea.

But one hungry fisherman, who had a large family to feed, decided to try. He took a line and a hook. He went to the water's edge, threw in the line, and stood battling on the sands. Hours passed and at last he felt a pull. Quickly, with all of his strength, he pulled the fish in. One little fish, but it was enough. He raced to the palace, holding the fish high. The palace guards let him in at once, but then he came to the king's door where the chamberlain stopped him.

"Let me pass, I must give the fish to the king," cried the fisherman.

"Only if you give me half of your reward," demanded the man.

"I cannot give you half, I have a large family," replied the fisherman. "Perhaps a tenth?"

"One half or you shall not go in," said the chamberlain with his fiercest look. At last the poor fisherman agreed and went inside.

Overjoyed, the king sent the fish at once to the royal kitchen. Then he turned to the fisherman and asked, "And what do you wish as your reward? Jewels, gold, a new home?"

"No sir, only 20 lashes."

"You must be joking," said the king. "You mean 20 elephants, or 20 fine gems?"

"No sir, only 20 lashes."

The king grew confused and a little upset, but the fisherman seemed determined. So the king took his cane and started to hit the fisherman lightly.

"Harder, sir, harder," said the man. Now the king grew annoyed and started to hit with more force. But as soon as he finished ten lashes, the fisherman jumped away.

"Did I hurt you too much?" asked the king in concern.

"No, sir, but my share is finished. Now you must give the Chamberlain his half," said the fisherman.

With a frown, the king demanded an explanation. The red-faced Chamberlain told him. But then he said, "Yet, your honour, I asked only for one half of the reward, not one half of the punishment, so I should not be whipped."

Now the king, although very angry, was puzzled, for he was a fair king. He quickly sent for Princess Learned-in-the-Law. She heard all aspects of the case. She looked at all three of the men then spoke, "Your honour, the fisherman and the Chamberlain were partners in a business – to supply a fish to you. But as partners, they are bound to share everything. Profit and loss, income and expenses, rewards and punishments are to be split equally, as both agreed."

Well pleased with the wise decision, the king proceeded to give ten strong strokes to the Chamberlain. Then he said, "Now your business is dissolved and you are fired." The Chamberlain left the palace in disgrace and the king happily appointed the clever fisherman to be the next Chamberlain. Then, at last, with a smile, the king sat down to enjoy his fish.

talk about
Good, old-fashioned
common sense.

The Philippines

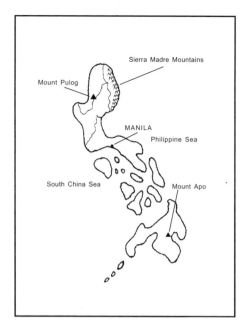

The island nation of the Philippines is an archipelago of over 7,000 islands in the Pacific Ocean, with mountains, coastal lowlands and many small rivers. Its salubrious temperate climate and its location attracted several colonisers, including the Spanish, the Japanese and the Americans. A combination of indigenous and foreign rule has led to a vibrant cultural mix, with Christianity the dominant religion. The national language is Filipino (based on Tagalog), although English is an official language as well. Traditional arts include weaving, metal work, pottery, and woodcarving. A rich oral literary tradition is shared, often with music, and dance forms are many. The most popular is the *tinikling* dance where dancers skillfully skip over bamboo sticks, to imitate a bird avoiding bamboo traps. Games, like the one below, are popular. These anecdotes, of play and pets, come from Cynthia Mejia-Giudici, who often heard her mother, Concolacion, tell true stories of growing up in 1930s in Pagasinan province, before and after the Japanese came.

Growing Up

A plate of rice spread above the town.

stars

ISA...DWA...TATLO...APAT...lima...anum..pitu...walo...sham...samplo..." Someone is counting to ten in Pangasinan dialect, in the moonlight, for 'Kick the Can'. But why would a Filipino version of Hide and Seek be given an English name? Did you know that the Philippines was ruled by the United States for almost fifty years (1898-1946)? That is why many Filipinos learned English in school.

Mom told me that to play this game, you needed good hiding spots and a can. The can was placed at 'home base', near the feet of the counter — IT. If you were IT, you covered your eyes and counted while your friends scrambled in the dark for a hiding place. The can stayed still while you searched for the hiders. But as you searched, your friends would try to run up to the can and kick it. Kick it hard, so it would fly far from that spot.

Mom laughed when she told me about this game. She remembered how frustrating it was because sometimes the can was kicked far away and she'd have to hurry to get it back to home base. Meanwhile, her friends would sneak back to home base without being tagged, so they were safe. However, some took their time to run in even if the can was kicked far away. Why? Were they too far from the safety zone? Couldn't they hear the other children running in?

Maybe they were teenagers, who loved this game very much. Remember, it was played by the light of the moon. But some places remained dark no matter how bright the moonlight was. So in that darkness, couples would run off to steal a few kisses and hugs, returning sometimes long after the game was done. I wonder if, by chance, my mother was one of those couples sometimes!

Years later, one day my Auntie Florentina started yelling: "You're getting old. It's time to get married."

My mother thought Auntie was crazy. Her mother, my Lola Monica, was only 12 when she was

96

forced to marry my grandfather, Clemente, ten years older. My mother, Cion, was the rebellious one. She had her own plans (unusual for a young woman in 1940s Philippines, and which sometimes got her into trouble).

"What? I'm only 17," she would reply. And the two bickered so much about it that her Uncle Jose punished my mother.

"You're a hard-headed girl. *Ay a natnalasi*!" he would yell and hit her, until she decided that she would not accept the offer to marry her cousin.

"Why do I have to marry a relative? I don't really know him or even like him. I'm only 17. I will not marry him!" were her defiant words. Then she ran away to the city, Dagupan, where her brother-in-law helped her find work as a waitress.

At times, mom would return home to Mapandan to see her mother. Most of all she needed comfort from her two pets, a cat and a dog. When she returned home her cat would be purring softly at her legs and the dog would jump on her lap and lick her face. It was good to be home and have such a warm welcome.

The family would feed her pets with the table scraps. But one time there wasn't much food and the cat wasn't filled with scraps. Now, some days Lola Monica would gut a *bangus* (milkfish), clean it, and hang it out to dry, since dried fish, *maluus*, is a good protein supplement for meals of rice and vegetables.

So that day, Lola Monica discovered that the cat had jumped onto the window ledge and nibbled the drying maluus.

"Ay a natnalasi itong gato!" she cursed the cat. Then she took the cat, put it in a gunny sack, and walked far into the sugarcane fields. There she left it to feed off the stubble of the sugar cane stalks and on the rats that ran through the fields. This was harsh punishment for a hungry cat.

Mom cried and cried and thought Lola Monica was so cruel. But Lola Monica was worried about feeding her family of thirteen children (my mother was the youngest). And she must have thought, "How dare a cat eat my children's food!"

Luckily, there is a happy ending. A week later, mom's cat found its way home from the field almost two miles away.

How ecstatic my mother was! From then on she vowed to take extra care of her cat when she was home, and convinced her sisters to keep a special eye, too. They made sure to save a portion of their meal for the cat so that it would never have to nibble the drying maluus. And Lola Monica never had to take it to the sugarcane fields again, or to give it away to envious neighbours.

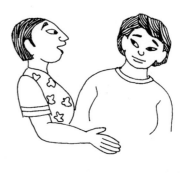

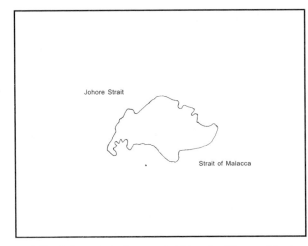

Singapore

A very small island nation, with 54 outlying islets, Singapore plays a vital role in the world's economy today. Once a quiet fishing village, it is now one of the world's largest ports. After the British and Japanese left in the middle of the 20ᵗʰ century, Singapore became part of the Federation of Malaysia. Then, in 1965, it became an independent nation, linked to the Malay Peninsula only by a causeway. Singapore's educational systems, its technological advancements, and its disciplined population have built a vital country, proud of its diversity and heritage. The four official languages are Malay, Chinese, Tamil, and English and stories are told in all of these. The two tales that follow are from two of Singapore's most popular storytellers: Rosemarie Somiah and Sheila Wee. In 'Kamut's Story', 'ayahanda' (a-yah-nde) and 'anakanda' (a-naknde) are classic Malay terms for father and daughter.

Kamut's Story

THERE ONCE WAS A PRINCESS who liked cats. She was a beautiful princess and, according to old Kamut in the village – who is said to have told this story many, many years before I was born — she was the daughter of the great, great, great, great-grandfather of the Sultan of his time.

One day, the proceedings of the royal court were interrupted by the Chief Minister. He bowed low, "Your Highness, the princess Puteri Mawar has a request."

The Sultan nodded, "The princess is my most precious jewel, my favourite flower. Let her come to me."

The princess came in carrying Kucinta her cat. She sat at the foot of her father's throne with the cat nestled in her lap. Dressed in the finest clothes, the princess's silky black hair shone and her smooth skin glowed. Pearls, rubies and sapphires gleamed from the chains and bracelets that adorned her neck and arms. The gems in the rings on her fingers sparkled as she stroked Kucinta.

The ministers dared not look too hard. It was said that any one of the rings on her fingers alone could buy a whole kingdom!

"Ayahanda,' began the princess, "why am I not allowed to swim in the river any more?"

"Anakanda, my beloved daughter, you know how dangerous the river can be."

"But, I am a good swimmer," said the princess.

"Sang Buaya, the crocodile, lurks in the river," warned her father.

"I am not afraid of a silly old crocodile!" responded the princess.

"You have heard the tales of robbers and pirates that roam the islands…" said her worried father.

"But the river flows just beside the palace," responded the princess. "What harm can come to me? Ayahanda, it is such a hot day! I fear this heat will scorch my skin and wither my beauty and...you know how I love to swim in the river!" Well, princesses will have their way and so did she.

Soon she was making her way to the river. Her attendants spread her clothes on the bushes by the river and laid her jewellery on silken cloths on the ground. They knew no one from the kingdom would dare come near.

Kucinta circled the princess curiously, its long tail held high. Suddenly, the princess had an idea. She took the precious rings off her fingers and slipped them onto the cat's tail. "You are my closest companion, Kucinta. You are as beautiful as a princess yourself. Keep my rings safe!" Then she knotted the end of the tail and slipped into the cool waters of the river, followed by her attendants. Kucinta wandered around and settled down for a nap.

Now, it happened that some pirates from a neighbouring island had been lurking in the area. Hiding in the bushes, they watched carefully till the princess and her attendants were some distance from the banks. Then, they sneaked out to steal the jewels.

But, Kucinta the cat had heard the rustling in the bushes. With its stomach and tail held low, it crept away stealthily into the long grass.

Before the princess and her attendants, out in the river, saw what had happened or could do anything about it, the pirates had escaped with most of the jewels. Everything was gone – except the rings still safe on Kucinta's tail!

The Sultan was relieved that his precious daughter was safe. But the princess did feel sorry. "Kucinta kept my rings safe, but look Father, its tail is bent and will not be straight again!"

"Kucinta has served you well," said the Sultan. "Let the knot in its tail be forever known as a mark of distinction – an honour – for loyalty and service to the kingdom."

And so it has been from that day on till today, to those who have heard this story. And, if you look at the cats that roam around Singapore today, you will find that most of them still carry that mark of honour — the knot in the tail!

Raja Suran's Expedition to China

LONG AGO there was a king. His name was Raja Suran and he ruled over all of India. But he wanted to be the most powerful king in the world. He made the princes of nearby countries bow down to him, pay him taxes of rice and gold, and say he was the most powerful king. But the Emperor of China refused to obey and so Raja Suran angrily vowed to invade China. He soon gathered a huge army from every part of his empire. The army was so big that it was impossible to count the number of soldiers, impossible to count the number of weapons, impossible to count the numbers of horses and elephants.

But Raja Suran had a slight problem. He wasn't exactly sure where China was. He thought that it was in the south, so he led his army through Thailand and further south into Malaysia. People said that wherever the army passed, forests were flattened, rivers dried up, and mountains trembled. People said it took six months for the army to pass by a single village. They kept on marching, month after month, until they stood looking across the water to Singapore, called Temasek in those days. Here they built rafts to ferry them over but they soon reached the Southern Sea and could go no further.

Raja Suran realised he would now have to travel by sea to reach China. So his men built hundreds of strong ships. Since he still didn't know which way to go, he sent men off in every direction.

Now, his journey had not been a secret. Traders of spices and aromatic woods who sailed the coast heard of the Raja's plan. They told their friends about the huge army looking for the route to China. Their friends told their friends, and their friends told their friends, until eventually someone told the Emperor of China himself. He was very worried and he and his ministers thought all day and all night about how to stop the army. Then, just as dawn was breaking, the Chief Minister burst out laughing. "Oh yes, I know a very good plan," he cried. And when the Emperor heard it, he smiled for the first time in days and said, " Yes, that is a fine plan. Go prepare everything needed."

And so the Chief Minister went down to the harbour to find a ship to sail to Temasek. But he didn't look for the best ship, the fastest ship, the newest ship. Oh no! He searched until he found the oldest ship – its planks well worn, its sails yellow with age. The other ministers were very puzzled. They were even more puzzled when the Chief Minister chose the oldest men he could find for sailors. Some were so old they could hardly walk and had to be carried onto the ship. "Old men, sailing an old ship; the Chief Minister's gone crazy," the people said.

Then he ordered that huge old fruit trees should be dug up, planted into pots and carried onto the deck of the ship. Lastly, he called for all the sewing needles in the city. Servants put all the rusty needles into sacks and by nightfall they loaded 50 sacks of rusty needles. Everyone was sure the Chief Minister and the Emperor had gone crazy. An old ship, with old sailors, old fruit trees and old rusty needles – how was that going to save them from the terrible army of Raja Suran?

The Emperor and the Chief Minister heard the whispers, but they just smiled as they waved the ship off on its journey. A few weeks later it arrived in Temasek. When the Raja's look-outs spotted the old ship limping into the harbour, with huge fruit trees growing on its deck and a crew of old grandfathers, they couldn't stop laughing. Soon everyone had heard about the strange ship and Raja Suran came to look, then ask, "Where have you come from? What country has such old sailors?"

One of the sailors spoke up, "We have come from China. When we set out, we were all strong young men – carrying a cargo of fruit tree seeds and shiny new swords. But it took us so long to get here that we have grown old, the seeds have become trees, and the swords have rusted away to the size of needles." Then he opened a sack of needles and as Raja Suran gazed down at the rusty needles, he sighed. If China was that far away he would be an old man before he got there, his soldiers would be old too – too old to fight. No it was not worth it. He would leave Temasek and send his army back to India, to find other, closer lands to conquer.

So Raja Suran gave the order for that huge army to turn around and march back the way it came to India. And so, thanks to a clever trick, China was safe again.

Thailand

Thai means 'freedom' in the native Tai (or Thai) language; it is also the name of the dominant ethnic group in Thailand. The name fits, for Thailand is the only country in Southeast Asia that was never colonised by European powers. Thailand has mountains in the north, the Khorat Plateau in the east, the Chao Phraya river valley in the central lowlands and the Kra Isthmus in the south. Thailand's robust economy is based on exports of tin, timber, rubber, natural gas and minerals. *Muay Thai* or Thai boxing is the national sport, while its rich arts include silk weaving, distinctive architecture and refined mural painting. Thai cuisine, now widely popular outside of Thailand too, is known for its balance of five fundamental flavours in each dish or in the overall meal. Theravada Buddhism is still central to Thai identity today. Most Thai men will spend some time in a Buddhist monastery, and children are raised with stories like this to help develop positive qualities.

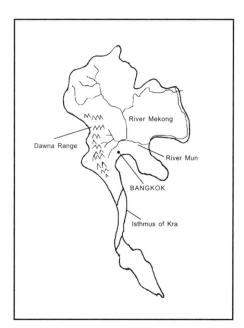

The Magic of Respect

ONCE IN THAILAND, a poor man travelled, working for what little money he could find. One day, in a quiet city, a beggar in rags asked for food. The young man happily shared his rice with him.

As the man was leaving, the beggar took his hand and said, "You have been kind to me. So I will give you a magic spell. It will help you later on. But if I teach it to you, I am your teacher and you must respect me all your life."

The man agreed at once and soon learned the wonderful magic. Now, if he wished to produce a fruit, he had only to say the magic words, blow gently on some water, pour the water on a fruit tree. At once, the fruit would bloom.

With this wonderful secret, he travelled from place to place, astounding people and earning fine rewards.

One cool winter day, he sat sipping tea in a rich city. All at once, he heard that the king had offered a huge reward to anyone who could find a mango for the pregnant queen, who craved it. But of course, no one could bring the fruit, for it grew only in summer.

The man went at once to the palace and offered his service. With the king, queen, and guards following him, the man asked for a bowl and water, then went to a mango tree. After he said his magic words, he blew on the water, and poured it on the tree. In moments, the most beautiful mango appeared and was given graciously to the queen. She was overjoyed and the man was well rewarded.

From that day on, he lived well in a new house that he built. He didn't need to use his secret any longer and simply enjoyed his wealth.

But one day, the king called to the man.

"I wish a mango now, in this winter," said the king. "And I also wish to know who taught you this wonderful magic. Tell me the name of your teacher, then give me a mango, and I will make you richer than you can imagine."

We swallow it and live,
But it can swallow us
and we die.

Water

101

Now the man was suddenly ashamed of the beggar who had taught him. So he lied and said he had learned it from a holy sage in the forest.

However, when he went to the mango tree, said the words, blew on the water, and poured it on the tree, nothing at all happened. He tried again and again to produce a fruit, but the tree remained bare and quiet.

"What is wrong?" demanded the king at last. And so, with his head bowed, the man finally told the truth. The king was furious at the man's lack of respect for his teacher. He took all of the man's wealth away and banished him from the kingdom.

Thus, again, the man found himself walking from town to town, seeking work, even begging for rice at times. But at least he now realised the power of respect.

talk about
Remembering – old friends, old times. Pride and prejudice.

Vietnam

Vietnam is a land of diversity: with densely forested highlands and mountains, the river deltas of the Red River and the Mekong, and coastal lowlands. Although Buddhism is most popular, a range of other religions are found, from local ones – Cao Dai and Hoa Hao – to Christianity, Islam and animism. Vietnamese is the dominant language, and the Kinh (Viet) people make up nearly 90 per cent of the population, with 53 minority groups (and many languages) making up the rest. One unique Vietnamese art is water puppetry, performed in shallow water to the vibrant sounds of Vietnamese instruments. The Vietnamese are also proud of their literary heritage: the *Tale of Kieu* is a national treasure, often quoted and known by all. Although Vietnam has a long history of invasion from both neighbouring China and Western powers, Vietnam now is at peace and building up its economy. The hard-working, studious Vietnamese are moving ahead, while keeping the strong, family-centred values shown in this favourite tale of the Lunar New Year.

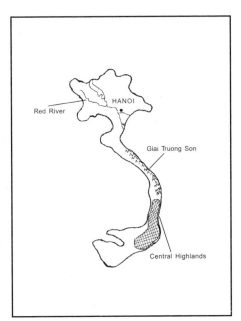

Bahn Day, Bahn Chung

ONCE IN VIETNAM, there lived a wise old king. After years of hard work, he knew he would soon leave this world. Since he had many sons, he announced one day that a contest would decide the next ruler.

"My sons," he said when they stood before him. "I may die soon without warning, so I must choose the next king by giving you a problem to solve. New Year approaches, the time to present the best offerings to our respected ancestors. Thus I will make king the one who can find the most excellent food to honour them."

Immediately, the different sons set off in different ways seeking food wondrous enough to win the contest. Some went to the seas; others hunted through the woods. Each was confident that he would become king — all except for the youngest son.

"How can I find the best food?" he wondered. "I am too young to go far away searching. What shall I bring?" He thought and thought and at last went to sleep, sad and discouraged.

But in his sleep he had a dream. A god appeared to him.

"My son," said the god, "the best food is one which everyone loves and eats — sticky rice. And the good deeds of our ancestors are as great as the heavens and the earth. So make good sticky rice into two fine shapes to honour the ancestors: a round cake to show the heavens, and a square one to stand for the earth."

In the morning the boy awoke very excited and confident. He had some good sticky rice pounded well, then shaped the rice flour into two rice cakes, wrapped them with leaves, and steamed them. One was like a circle and he called it Banh Day, while the square one he named Banh Chung. Then he took his rice cakes before the king's high throne.

Magnificent smells swirled through the air as his brothers brought

It waves a flag and fans itself.

An elephant.

103

rich soups, rare fish and wild mushrooms, thin and thick noodles in spicy sauces. The king nibbled and tasted a little from each dish.

"These are all very fine," he said. "But which one is truly the best?"

Just then, his youngest son came up.

"Father, please try these cakes now," he said with a bow.

The king stared at the very plain-looking, white rice cakes while the other princes laughed.

"How can this be the best food? It is only rice. And why is it so strangely shaped?" asked the king.

"Father, my rice cakes are made from rice since the simplest food can also be the best. Everyone can enjoy rice, whether rich or poor. And the cakes are shaped to help us honour our ancestors. The round shape stands for the heavens, the square shape for the earth itself. Both of these are to be offered to the ancestors, who are as important as the heavens and the earth."

The king listened to his wise son. He tasted the rice cakes with both mind and tongue. He was well pleased.

"I have found the best ruler," he said at last to all those gathered there. Soon after, the boy became king, and his rule was rich in both wisdom and simple kindness to all.

talk about
What is wisdom?
What is knowledge?

VISUAL ARTS

MALAY KITES

Malay kites are known for their beauty and flight, but they are not the fighting kites popular in South Asia. Some of the Malay kites are made to fly, and some are made for decoration, with vivid, cut paper designs. Students can decorate Malay type kites to brighten up any room.

Materials

Large sheets of paper and colours
Bits of coloured tissue and shiny paper
Scissors/blades, paste
Kite pattern

Method

❖ Copy the kite pattern on the board for students to copy, or make copies to give out. Have one kite for each small group.
❖ Find out who flies kites in the class. Ask them if anyone has heard about kites in Malaysia. Tell them the names of popular kite shapes there to stimulate their imaginations: cat kite, moon kite, quail kite, frog kite, peacock kite, fairy godmother kite, hawk kite, and the fishnet of wisdom kite
❖ Have each group cut (or draw) a kite outline.
❖ Using any of these traditional Malay images (or their own ideas), students then decorate kites with any materials on hand: a central flower (from which vines, leaves, and flowers sprout), cloud patterns, wood carvings, local vegetation (including frangipani and yam flowers), floral borders from batik fabrics, sharks' teeth borders.
❖ Hang kites from a string, place on the wall, or let them float in a window to cheer up any room.

WHEELS OF STORY

In lovely Suan Mok monastery in southern Thailand years ago, I saw very beautiful, large round stones carved to tell the stories of the Buddha's past lives. Students can't carve in stone, but they can use a large circle to tell a story.

Materials

Large paper – can be newspaper – cut in big circles
Paint, marker colours, or bright papers (all sizes, scrap, magazine pictures, tissue paper, etc.)
Scissors/blades, paste

Method

❖ Discuss the ways that pictures help tell stories (using examples from the intros and students' experiences).
❖ Have students think of one story in the region. Working in small groups, they then design a circular way of telling the story, placing characters, settings, story objects, scenes in any design or order they wish.
❖ Give each group a large circle. They can either colour directly on it, or paste cut out/torn shapes for parts of the story.
❖ When their group circle story is done, students can practice telling the story together, using the circle.
❖ Circles can be displayed, as students tell stories.

ELEPHANT MOSAIC

Each region has an animal that seems to represent the area, or animals that are so well loved or known there. One of the popular animals in much of South and Southeast Asia is the elephant. Making a lovely, big elephant mural is a great class project.

Materials

Newspapers
Small papers, cloth scraps, bangle bits, and paste

Method

❖ Tell the class that they will be decorating big paper elephants the next day, in a mosaic style. Ask them to bring small colour paper or cloth scraps, bits of foil or bangles, old stamps, and other things to use.
❖ Find out how many students have seen elephants and where they've seen them. Ask for descriptions.

- ❖ Divide students in small groups and give each group a large piece of a newspaper.
- ❖ Have each group cut or carefully tear their paper in the shape of a big elephant.
- ❖ Now have students cut or tear the papers and cloth scraps, etc. into very small pieces.
- ❖ Using gum/paste, let each group make a mosaic of these small pieces, to decorate their elephant.
- ❖ Hang or tack them up in a great elephant parade.

VERBAL/WRITTEN ARTS

TALES OF A WATER VILLAGE

The small, prosperous nation of Brunei has the largest water village in Southeast Asia, in existence for over 1300 years. It is a unique world of its own, with over 3000 structures and all the conveniences: air conditioning, Internet, plumbing, etc. Students can create story parts about this unusual setting.

Materials

Description of water village below
Pen and pencil, slate and chalk

Methods

- ❖ Discuss the role of a setting to give mood to a story. Ask students to describe some of the settings found in other stories in the book. They may note that in some stories, the setting is very vague, while in others, it is important to the plot and very clear.
- ❖ Tell them that they will now work with a special, unique Southeast Asian setting: Kampong Ayer, Brunei's Water Village.
- ❖ Read the description of the village, then ask them to use their imaginations to write more details about (a) the setting, (b) a character there, or (c) a problem that could come up there.
- ❖ Share students' writing, as rough sketches. If some wish to elaborate, invite them to develop a whole story.

Source Material

This village of over 30,000 people looked like several enormous clusters of houses on stilts, all in the middle of the Brunei River...(at dawn) the clattering footsteps of children and commuters along rickety wooden walkways were joined by the rumble of motorised water taxis as they ferried people to the nearby shore... After the morning commute subsided, women began to drape the wooden balconies of the village with freshly washed batik sarongs and children's clothes (next to cascades of orchids). Woven mats were set out and spread with prawns, small fish and *krupuk* crackers. Beneath the houses, open boats bobbed in the river. Little boys lowered crab pots from bedroom windows. Telephones rang, cats and lizards took up sunny positions on the wooden walkways, and the sounds of hammers, saws, and boiling teakettles indicated that another day was in full swing in Kampong Ayer. (Hansen: 1995,32)

SOUTHEAST ASIAN RIDDLES

In the many lands of Southeast Asia are many riddles. These clever metaphors and mini-poems are great fun to share: they teach imagination, language, and culture. Use the following idea to spark interest in these traditional riddles, and collect more whenever you can.

Materials

Riddles on P. 107, along with your favourites

Method

- ❖ Ask students to share some of their favourite riddles with you. You may find that they are the newer joke types of riddles, but that's okay.
- ❖ After they're shared a few, give them some of the ones on p. 107. Read the introduction about traditional riddles, if it's appropriate for the age of your students.
- ❖ When they've solved some and got the idea of these traditional riddles, challenge students to come up with an original one of their own. Have them work in small groups or with partners to help brainstorm.

- Call the class back together after they've had enough time. Invite them to share their new riddles.
- If you'd like, you can later ask them to collect some older riddles from family members or neighbours and share those as well.

Source Material

Traditional, or true, riddles at times start with a formula or question, but often they do not. The simplest riddle describes an object fairly directly, with imagination: 'One animal with two tails' is, of course, an elephant.

Other riddles describe one image and ask the listener to jump from that description to the riddle's answer, which will have similar characteristics. The riddle, 'A red snake wanders amidst white stones', doesn't describe a real snake, the answer is instead the red tongue that wanders amidst white teeth! 'Two sisters look out' describes two eyes!

Filipino

A nice house has walls full of holes. *spider's web*
He pulled out a stick and it was followed by a snake. *needle, thread*
A small hill having seven holes. *head*

Vietnamese

Five boys use two poles to chase white water buffaloes into the cave. *hand, rice, chopsticks*
It's green outside but white inside. It's hard for a man to get at it. *coconut*

Indonesian

When you close this fence completely, nobody can enter. *teeth*
In this stone, is a pond. *coconut*

SONGS/GAMES

Many children in Southeast Asia grow up without fancy toys, but still have fun playing with simple materials and games. Lat, the talented, popular Malay cartoonist, in his book, *Kampung Boy*, shares a range of homemade pleasures in the kampung community he grew up in – from kites to slingshots to marbles and pitching games using cigarette boxes and more. Here are two other games to try.

THREE HOUSES FROM MYANMAR

Materials

Outside playfield, chalk/stone for lines

Method

- Three large squares are drawn with chalk or made with sticks/stone on the ground.
- Students are counted out by the first rhyme until only two are left. Then the second rhyme is said and the child left is IT.
- All students then quickly run off while IT tries to catch them. Whenever they stand in a house, they are safe.
- After several children are caught, the game starts again with the rhymes and a new IT.

Source Material

Made of lines
Three houses
Just for us
Off you go
Save yourself and run

Palm juice
Palm sugar
Palm sugar lumps
Bend over, take some
Now, follow me.

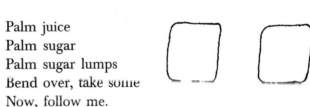

DE DE UM (from Vietnam)

Materials

Field, with home base at one end, start line at the other. Across the centre, a long rectangle, for IT, is marked – half a metre in length and running across the width of the game field

Method

- One person, the Catcher, holds his hand palm up. The other players each point their fingers at the Catcher, as he calls out slowly, De De Um. At the sound of the last word, the Catcher tries to grab any finger.
- The first caught is IT and has to stand in ITs box. All the others stand at startline.

- Students must run across room and touch base. Then they must crouch down and cross arms to hold opposite earlobes. In this position, they return across room to safety.
- IT tries to catch children as they cross ITs territory. Students try to use strategy and distract IT. First one caught becomes the next Catcher.

Note: To make it trickier, you can say the tenth or the fifth person caught, etc., instead of the first.

NATURE/SCIENCE

SURVIVAL RADIO

Two very important natural resources are found in Southeast Asia: the Mekong River that winds through much of the region, supporting a range of human, plant, and animal life, and the wonderful rainforests. Both are in danger as people seek to dam the river, and clear the forests – for palm oil plantations, lumber, and other products. Students can learn more about protecting these precious resources as they start with the rainforests.

Materials

Research materials online or in books
Facts below

Methods

- After students have read stories from Southeast Asia, ask them what else they know of the region and its natural wealth. If Internet access is available, ask them to do some research on rainforests in the area.
- Share the facts below about Brunei's rainforest. Note the incredible diversity in the rainforests and that many indigenous people depend on these disappearing resources.
- Remind students that all rainforests have similar riches. Discuss what will happen when rainforests are destroyed; think of all the plants, animals, and humans that will be affected.
- In small groups, have students create a radio programme – Save the Rainforests – with facts on Southeast Asian rainforests, stories about them, problems facing them from logging, etc., beneficial projects and studies now under way, and suggestions for ways to help (writing letters

to companies clearing rainforests or finding what products are made from rainforests and conserving them to stop demand, etc.)
- Share the programme with your school, neighbourhood. Write it down and send it online or to a youth magazine.

Source material

A single acre (4000 square metres) of tropical rainforest can be home to about 20,000 different kinds of insects and 100 varieties of plants; a typical 1000-hectare area (2560 acres) may house 1500 species of flowering plants, 750 kinds of trees, 400 bird species and 150 varieties of butterflies.

In fact, about one-quarter of the prescription medicines on the market today are derived from plants, but less than one per cent of tropical rainforest species have been examined for possible medicinal value. Seventy per cent of plants identified as useful in the treatment of cancer are found only in rainforests – which are being destroyed worldwide at a rate of 32 hectares (80 acres) every minute.
(Eigeland: 1992, 4)

ALL GIVING

In much of Southeast Asia, the sugar palm is known as a life-giving tree, for every part of it is used for something. Students will identify other similar givers in their region.

Materials

List below

Method

❖ Tell students that the sugar palm of Southeast Asia is a rich tree, helping humans in many ways.

❖ See if they can identify the various gifts it gives. Help them, if needed, by referring to list above.

❖ Ask students to think of giving plants and animals in your country (e.g. coconut tree, camel, cow, etc.). List the name and every product/service it gives.

❖ If desired, finish with an art project: chart or poster showing uses of one plant or animal. Be thankful!

Source Material

List of uses for sugar palm:
Edible oil, sweets, leaves used for thatching/mats, leaf stalk fibres twined to make ropes, dried shells and leaf stalks used for fuel, trunks used as poles in construction or as timber, trunk of tree hollowed and used as a boat.

THINGS TO THINK ABOUT

WISDOM AND THE LAW

Although Princess Learned-in-the-Law did not actually live, law students in Myanmar years ago were given her legendary cases to help them learn law. Students can think like the wise judges of the past and try to solve local problems.

Method

❖ Discuss the case solved by Princess Learned-in-the-Law.

❖ Remind students that although lawyers and judges today refer to many cases and many laws, there is also a way to discover the truth through problem-solving, as she did.

❖ Brainstorm as a class some specific problems that might come before a judge in your neighbourhood: cases of theft, arguments over property, people cheating others, child abuse, child labour.

❖ Divide class into small groups.

❖ Ask each group to choose one problem and to make up a specific case: with a defendant, a plaintiff, a judge, and lawyers.

❖ Have them make up a small drama acting out their case, with arguments on both sides and a judge's final decision.

TEACHING TALES

The Thai story of a mango and the Vietnamese tale of the rice cakes are fine illustrations of small stories with big meanings. These types of teaching tales have been used for centuries. Give your students a chance to share some more.

Materials

A story or two from your memory/reading

Method

❖ Discuss with students what these two stories talk about. Mention other small teaching tales from other sections in the book.

❖ For homework, ask them each to find at least one short, interesting tale, with a value, from parents, neighbours, teachers, or a book.

❖ Start the session off with your own story, then have students take turns sharing their tales.

· These short stories are usually easy to find and to tell, so they give students good storytelling practice. Enjoy.

Stories and Activities
West Asia

Mediterranean Sea

ANKARA

Turkey

Lebanon

BEIRUT

Israel TEL AVIV

Syria

Caspian Sea

DAMASCUS

JERUSALEM

Palestine

AMMAN

Jordan

BAGHDAD

TEHRAN

Turkmenistan

Iraq

Kuwait

Iran

Afghanistan

Red Sea

•RIYADH

KUWAIT CITY

Saudi Arabia

MANAMA

Bahrain

Pakistan

Qatar

DOHA

ABU DHABI

UAE

Persian Gulf

MUSCAT

SANA'A

Yemen

Oman

Arabian Sea

THE REGION

WEST ASIA, A REGION WITH SHARP CONTRASTS as well as strong ties, has changed dramatically in the last century. Incredible oil wealth (Saudi Arabia's land holds 25 per cent of all known world oil reserves) and/or industrial development have helped nations like Qatar and U.A.E. to join the circle of wealthy nations, while others like Yemen and Syria still struggle. The faith of Islam and strong family values help to create a certain unity in the region, although rules and conservatism vary, and Turkey has a secular government that hopes to join the European Union.

Geographically, varied natural features are found: there are the two great rivers, the Nile and the Tigris-Euphrates, and the lowest point on earth (417 metres below sea level), the very salty Dead Sea. Yet it is the desert that truly defines much of the region. About 80 per cent of West Asia's land area is classified as semi-desert or desert, while forest areas cover only about four per cent. Desert dwellers have adapted to the challenging environment: clustering around springs and water sources, developing very clever irrigation systems, carefully monitoring water usage when necessary. For long years, the camel has provided the ideal means of transport for such a desert climate – its double rows of eyelashes protect it from the sun and its body chemistry enables it to live without water or food for up to seven days.

Across the sands have come pilgrims on the blessed Hajj pilgrimage since the early days of Islam in the seventh century. Today, workers from South and Southeast Asia also come; some West Asian countries have very high percentages of foreign workers. The nomadic Bedouins, too, have lived for centuries in the region, with their fierce loyalty to clan and tribe, their hospitality, and their love of freedom. Indeed, human history began early in this region: the world's earliest civilisation is believed to have started in Sumer, now in Iraq, around 6000 BCE, and Damascus in Syria is said to be the world's oldest continuously inhabited settlement (sharing honours in some lists with Arbil in Iraq, Byblos in Lebanon, and others).

The land that is now Iran was also the home of empires, wealth, and culture – its early history is recorded in the great *Shahnama* epic, shared to this day. As civilisations grew there, the products of West Asia, including incense and pearls, were eagerly traded in routes by land and by sea. Later, as Islam spread, great cultural centres sprang up in this region. For centuries, these lands were more advanced in the sciences and arts than was Europe; Greek learning was preserved in this region when it was eclipsed in its home.

The glories of empires like the Ottoman were indeed dazzling: lands were conquered by the Janissaries (an incredibly disciplined infantry), great mosques were built, the arts flourished. By the late seventeenth century, however, advances in the West changed the balance. Then from the West (especially Great Britain and France) came the greater might of weaponry and the greed of imperial powers, which often came first to trade then stayed to control. After many struggles in the twentieth century and under the leadership of Turkey's Kemal Ataturk, Egypt's Gamal Abdel Nasser, and others, the region slowly became independent and new countries were formed.

Daily life in the region today is regulated by the call to prayer five times a day, while the passing of months is watched carefully to prepare for Ramzan, the month of fasting. Women lead varied lives in West Asia: some wear veils (by their choice, at times), most vote, and many work outside the home. Extended families are still quite common and children are very welcome. Most of those children now go to school, and many still read or hear stories just like the ones here.

. . . and its STORIES

Even before the advent of Islam, the Arabian cultures boasted a rich tradition of poetry sung or recited. Then came Islam, with its prophets and teachings. Storytelling grew for some time, but faced problems with its material (for it wasn't serious literature) and with the extremely theatrical styles of some tellers. Today, several storytelling forms can be found but none seem to be thriving.

In Turkey, as in other areas of West Asia, the coffeehouse provided a receptive, male storytelling audience for years, although less so today. Turkish women told tales in homes and at afternoon teas. However, the traditions of women's storytelling in homes are fading along with the men's traditions. Also in Turkey, the *asik*, or 'lover poet', is called to his profession in a dream where a white-haired dervish introduces him to an exquisite girl, who will be his lifelong love. The two pledge their love, then he awakes to spend the rest of his life searching for her, singing songs in her praise that become the romances he shares in the coffeehouses. (Walker: 1966, xiii) And far outside the cities, when herding families needed to take flocks to summer pastures, they shared tales then, too, since during those three months there was little entertainment.

In long ago Iran, kings called upon epic storytellers to teach kingly behaviour through stories. Centuries later, the *naghal* teller played the roles of different characters as he narrated stories, often in coffeehouses. Epics of romance and heroism, along with religious narratives, were popular.

Since many storytellers were non-literate, they did not all tackle the *Shahnama*, that grand national epic of Iran's past kings, written by the poet Firdausi (Hakim Abul-Qasim Firdausi Tusi – also spelled Firdawsi and Ferdowsi). Then, around 1929, by order of the Shah, all the storytellers in coffeehouses had to tell only the *Shahnama*.

A visual form of storytelling, *pardehdari*, was also popular in Iran, especially to share the stories of the Shia imams: the central figure was usually the martyr Hussein. As a large, painted scroll was unrolled against a wall in the street, the stories would be told by an imposing figure in a long robe and fez, who narrated while using a cane to point. It was a form not encouraged by the authorities, though, and it soon was found only in rural, out-of-the-way villages.

Today, the future is not encouraging for these storytelling forms in Iran. When the great Murshid Zariri of Iran was invited to tell the *Shahnama* at a hotel, rich people and tourists came eagerly. "However," he said, "none of them listened to the story. It was as though they had no idea what the *Shahnama* was..." (Omidsalar: 1999,337).

In Syria, the *hakawati* storyteller also tells in a coffeehouse, sitting or standing, book in one hand, cane or sword in the other, reading the text or reciting from memory and interjecting poems, jokes and commentary. In its heyday, a known teller could pack a house of 200 and use accents with great facility. They say that a famous hakawati, Abu 'Ali Abouba, once went to a new doctor, complaining of melancholy. The doctor, not recognizing him, said, "You need to see the hakawati Abouba, who will cheer you up." "But," said the patient sadly, "I *am* Abouba!" (Aziz: 1996,15)

The hakawati tells tales of heroes: Sultan Baybars, the Banu Hilal Arabs, Prince Antar. Today, the art suffers as the coffeehouses that supported it lose their regular audiences or shut down completely.

Bahrain

The island nation of Bahrain, which means 'two seas' in Arabic, is the smallest Arab country, and yet the most prolific book publisher in the Arab world. Its strategic location in the Persian Gulf along with its fertile lands, fresh water and pearls, attracted early settlers. Pearl diving declined last century, but the traditional songs, fidjeri, of the divers have become quite popular today. Arabic is the official language and Islamic heritage is evident in all parts of life, from crafts – intricate door carvings, weaving, filigree, boat building, pottery – to recitations from the *Qu'ran*. Bahrain also houses a special museum of the *Qu'ran* with magnificent priceless copies of the holy book from various places and times. The following small chain story, which shares the power of quiet charity, is not from the *Qu'ran* but from the sayings of Prophet Muhammad.

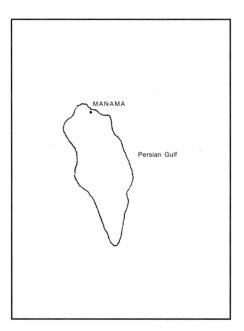

MANAMA

Persian Gulf

What God Said

THE ANGELS ASKED, "O God! Is there anything of Thy creation stronger than rocks?"

God said, "Yes, iron is stronger than rocks, for it breaks them."

The angels said, "O Lord! Is there anything of Thy creation stronger than iron?"

God said, "Yes, fire is stronger than iron, for it melts it."

And the angels said, "O Defender! Is there anything of Thy creation stronger than fire?"

God said, "Yes, water overcomes fire; it kills it and makes it cold."

Then the angels said, "O Lord! Is there anything of Thy creation stronger than water?"

God said, "Yes, wind overcomes water; it agitates it and puts it in motion."

They said, "O Our Cherisher! Is there anything of Thy creation stronger than wind?"

God said, "Yes, O children of Adam, giving alms; that is, those who give with their right hands and conceal it from their left, they overcome all."

Iran

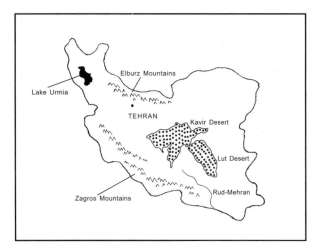

Iran's fertile lands, rich resources, and its strategic position have supported human civilisation for over 6000 years. Although various cultures have left their mark, the Persians and Azeris are the largest groups today, and Persian is the official language. The sole habitat for the endangered Asiatic cheetah, Iran has a mountainous rim, a high central basin with deserts, mountains, and small plains along both coasts. Iran has contributed much to science and to architecture, with its massive domes known for their beauty of form. A rich literary tradition includes the famous work, *Shahnama*, of Firdausi, which tells of Iran's early kings.

In the section below, brave young Sohrab has at last found his father, the great hero Rustam, but neither realises it. They see themselves only as enemies, and thus a terrible tragedy occurs on the battlefield.

On the Battlefield

Placed above, it makes greater things small.
Placed beside it, it makes small things greater.
In matters that count, it always comes first.
Where others increase, it keeps all things the same.

The number one.

Rustam went back to the field upset and pale
While, like a mad elephant, Sohrab,
With lasso on his arm and bow in hand,
Came in his pride and roaring like a lion.
When Rustam saw the look of his foe
He was amazed and gazing carefully,
Weighed in his mind the chances of the fight.
Sohrab, puffed up with youthful pride,
When he saw Rustam in his strength and grace,
Cried: "You who escaped the Lion's claw!
Why come now bravely to fight me? Speak!
Do you have some interest to seek?"
Then the two began
To wrestle...(until) Rustam clutched
That warrior-leopard by the head and neck,
Bent down the body of the bold boy,
Whose time was come, whose strength was gone.
And like a lion dashed him to the ground.
Then, knowing that Sohrab would not stay there,
Drew his sword
And thrust it into the chest of his brave son.
...Sohrab cried: "Ah! I am alone to blame,"
He said to Rustam, "You had luck and now
Others will mock me since I die so young.
My mother told me
How I should recognise my father Rustam.
I looked for him with love and die with that great wish.
Alas! It is all for nothing, for I have not seen him...

Yet my father will stand up for me always
Against all who wrong me."
Then Rustam grew most upset.
The world turned black, his body failed.
He sank on the ground and fainted, until
Awaking, he cried in pain:
"Where is the proof that you are Rustam's son?
For I am Rustam! Be my name forgotten."
He raved, his blood flowed, and with groans he plucked
His hair up by the roots, while at the sight
Sohrab sank and then cried:

"If you are Rustam, you have killed me wrongly,
for I asked you your name.
But nothing that I did would stir your love.
Undo my armour and see your jewel.
The drums beat at my gate, my mother came
With blood-stained cheeks and hurt to the heart
Because I left. She tied this jewel on mine arm
And said: 'Keep this jewel of your father's.'
But the fight is over now and
The son is nothing to his father."
When Rustam loosened
The armour and saw the gem he tore his clothes,
And cried: "Oh! my brave son loved by all
And killed by me!"
With dust upon his head
And tearstained face he tore his hair until
His blood ran down.
"Nay, this is worse and worse,"
Sohrab said, "But why weep? How will it help to kill yourself?"
...(battle sounds increase and Sohrab begs his father to stop the battle, and to set
free Sohrab's prisoner, then says...)
"I saw in you the signs that my mother
Described, but trusted not my eyes. The stars
Declared that I die by your hand.
I came like lightning and like wind I go.
In heaven I may look on you with joy."
Then Rustam choked, his heart was full of fire,
His eyes of tears. (After Sohrab dies,
Rustam tells his men of his awful deed,
And calls off the attack saying)...

"I have lost today
All strength and courage.
Fight not with the enemy;
I have done harm enough."

Listen a hundred times,
ponder a thousand
times, speak once.
– a Kurdish saying

117

Iraq

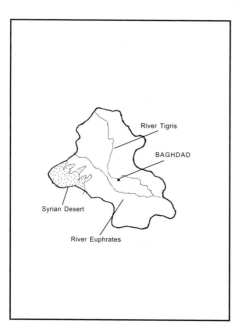

Iraq, historically known as Mesopotamia, was the cradle of the world's first known civilisation, nourished by two major rivers, the Tigris and the Euphrates. The Persians, the Arabs, and the Ottoman empires overran the land in the past, while a tragic conflict causes destruction and loss now. Arabic and Kurdish are official languages in this land of broad plains, with mountains bordering Iran and Turkey. Carpets, textiles, brass and copper work, palm tree products, leatherworks, and glass painting are some of Iraq's crafts. The oud and the rabab are important instruments, widely known to have originated here. Literary and spiritual pursuits were many in Iraq. Enjoy the tale of Rabi'a, a respected female Sufi of the eighth century, and sketch by the renowned writer Al-Jahiz. Today's tragedy is shared below through excerpts from a popular blog, 'Baghdad Burning' by a brave Iraqi woman.

The Real Work

What you give away, you keep.
– a Kurdish saying

ONE DAY, Hasan, a fellow (spiritual) seeker, saw Rabi'a as she stood near a lake. Suddenly, he threw his prayer rug on the surface of the water, and called, "Rabi'a, come! Let us pray two rak'as (cycles of prayer) here!"

"Hasan," Rabi'a replied calmly, "when you are showing off your spiritual goods in this worldly market, show something that your fellowmen cannot do."

Then she threw her prayer rug up into the air, where it stayed still on the wind. With a jump, she flew right to it. She looked down and cried, "Come up here, Hasan, where people can see us!"

Hasan, who was not as advanced spiritually, had nothing to say. Rabi'a then tried to console him.

"Hasan," she said, "what you did the fishes can also do. What I did the flies can also do. The real work is beyond both these tricks. One must apply one's self to that real work alone."

Nothing Wasted

Abu Sa'id used to forbid his servant to throw the garbage out, and even instructed her to collect the tenants' garbage and put it with his own. Then every so often he would sit down, and the servant would get a basket, tip out little heaps of rubbish in front of him, and he'd rummage through them one by one.

If he found some dirhams, a purse of housekeeping money, a dinar or a piece of jewellery, it is easy to guess what he did with it. Wool was destined to be collected up and sold to the makers of pack-saddles, and similarly with pieces of cloth. Rags were sold to tray and hardware merchants, pomegranate skins to dyers

118

and tanners, bottles to glassmakers, date-pits to gazelle-breeders, peach-pits to nurserymen, and nails and bits of old iron to blacksmiths.

Pieces of papyrus were destined for the paper-mill, and sheets of paper were used as stoppers for jars. Any bits of wood he sold to pack-saddle makers, bones were used for lighting the fire, and pottery fragments for new kilns, and stones were collected up for use in building.

The basket was then shaken to pack down the rubbish and put on one side to serve as fuel for firing the oven. Pieces of pitch were sold to a pitch merchant.

Baghdad Burning

3/26/04: And where are we now? Well, our governmental facilities have been burned to the ground by a combination of "liberators" and "Free Iraqi Fighter"; 50% of the working population is jobless and hungry; summer is looming close and our electrical situation is a joke; the streets are dirty and overflowing with sewage; our jails are fuller than ever with thousands of innocent people; we've seen more explosions, tanks, fighter planes and troops in the last year than almost a decade of war with Iran brought; our homes are being raided and our cars are stopped in the streets for inspection... journalists are being killed "accidentally" and the seeds of a civil war are being sown by those who find it most useful: the hospitals overflow with patients but are short on just about everything else — medical supplies, medicines and doctors; and all the while, the oil is flowing.

3/18/06: It has been three years since the beginning of the war that marked the end of Iraq's independence. Three years of occupation and bloodshed. Three years and the electricity is worse than ever. The security situation has gone from bad to worse. The country feels like it's on the brink of chaos once more – but a pre-planned, pre-fabricated chaos being led by religious militias and zealots...

And what role are the occupiers playing in all of this? It's very convenient for them, I believe...they can be the neutral foreign party trying to promote peace and understanding between people who, up until the occupation, were very peaceful and understanding...Even the most cynical war critics couldn't imagine the country being this bad three years after the war...God protect us from the fourth year.

talk about
Children and war.

Israel

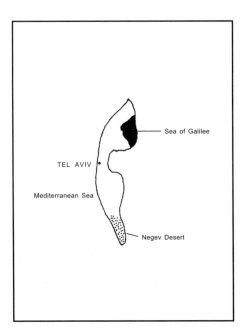

Israel came into being in 1948 when, after World War II, the British withdrew from Palestine, and the UN partitioned the area into Arab and Jewish states. Arabs rejected this arrangement and the region has been the scene of war and struggle for decades. Although small, Israel has four geographic regions: the northern hills, the Mediterranean coast, the Great Rift Valley, and the Negev Desert. Agricultural collectives, *kibbutzim*, were a bold experiment that helped to make the deserts bloom in Israel. Hebrew and Arabic are the official languages and most people follow Judaism in the world's only Jewish state, but there are Muslims as well. A range of art forms includes symphony orchestras, folk dances, embroidery, and a rich heritage of Jewish literature. This powerful poem by Tali Shurek, 13, who lived in Beer Sheva, shares the dream of many Israelis.

I spread a net,
but I'm not a fisherman.
What I catch in the net
is not a fish.

I'm a spider!

The Paint Box

I had a paint box –
Each colour glowing with delight:
I had a paint box, with colours
Warm and cool and bright.
I had no red for wounds and blood,
I had no black for an orphaned child,
I had no white for the faces of the dead,
I had no yellow for burning sands.
I had orange for joy and life,
I had green for buds and blooms,
I had blue for clear bright skies.
I had pink for dreams and rest.
I sat down
and painted
Peace.

talk about
Can children make
a difference?

120

Jordan

Jordan, independent since 1946, is a monarchy, and a country carved out of ancient lands, with its borders fixed earlier to accommodate the political needs of Great Britain. It has some 5,00,000 archaeological sites, including the great city of Petra. Most of the people are Arabs, with a significant minority of Bedouins; the major religion is Islam, and the official language is Arabic, although English is also spoken. Largely desert, the western part is fertile, producing citrus fruits, barley, lentils, and watermelons. *Dabkah* are popular group dances characterised by pounding feet on the floor to mark rhythm, while the *sahjah* is a well-known Bedouin dance. Abd Al-Rahman Munif, one of Egypt's most famous writers, remembers the exciting days of his youth in Amman in the two passages below. The second speaks of Yacoub Hashem, the mathematics teacher in the secondary school, known to all for his simple manner and his devotion to maths.

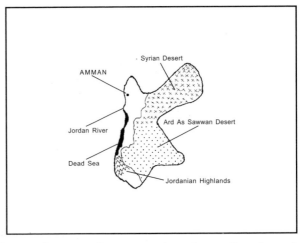

Memories of Amman

(THE CHILDREN) COULD STAND outside the shops of the knife and scissor sharpeners, who did not mind showing off their skill in front of the children!

They could stand outside Safadi bookshop and look through the window at the display of books which never changed.

They could watch the only petrol pump in town in the middle of King Faisal Street, as a glass cylinder was tilted by hand to fill up the petrol tank of one of the few cars in Amman.

They could stand outside the Aziziyeh shop to savour the smell of coffee and sweets, and to check the price of the Faber fountain pen.

They could pass through the Bukhariyah souk and scan the ground for things people had dropped.

Once he was walking in the souk near the Samman printing press, where the buses for Madaba used to stop. He was absorbed in a mathematical problem which he had been trying to resolve. Suddenly the beginning of a solution flashed into his mind, so he simply began to write symbols and numbers in the dust that was covering one of the buses. As he was busy writing, it was time for the bus to move. When he was warned of this, he paid for a seat on the bus to delay its departure so that he could copy the conclusions at which he had arrived."

"(Then, some say) that because time was so short, he was forced to board the bus and go to Madaba in the hope that he would get the opportunity of working further on the problem and finding the answer. However, the road was unpaved and more dust covered the partial solution he had written on the outside of the bus! And so the problem remained unsolved!"

Kuwait

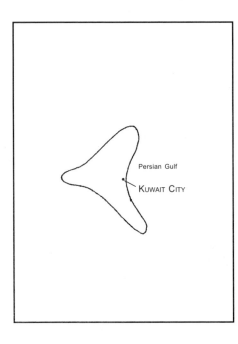

Persian Gulf

KUWAIT CITY

Largely nomadic in the past, the people of Kuwait today are settled in a land of flat desert, with no significant water supply. When oil wealth grew, though, Kuwait became the first Arab nation in the Persian Gulf to declare independence, in 1961. Many foreign workers have come over the past decades: Kuwait today has a foreign labour force of over 60 per cent. In 1990, Iraq invaded and Kuwait's economy was badly damaged, but it has regained its prosperity now. Education has been well funded, and Kuwait's literacy rate of 83 per cent is one of the highest in the Arab world. The *Dewaniya*, an important Kuwaiti institution, encourages learning, too, as a meeting place for men to discuss politics, business, and life. *Al-Fareesa* is a dance performed on certain holidays by women disguised as men and portraying a battle between a horseman and two attackers. Traditional Kuwaiti music is mostly performed by women in private, using hand-clapping or simple drums. Women also tell tales in their homes.

Pot of Meat

ONCE A POOR MAN lived with his three daughters and a small dog. Life was too hard and there was too little to eat. Then one day, the man found some meat to eat. After it started to cook, the four went to do their work. But one by one, they crept to the pot to sneak a little meat.

When the youngest girl saw this, she grew angry and suddenly took the whole pot and ran outside, with the dog following behind. On she ran, but soon the others discovered the missing pot and started to chase her. At last, their footsteps stopped; she and the dog were safe. But she was so tired that she lay down near a fence there and was soon asleep.

Now it so happened that the fence surrounded a fine palace. And the prince who lived there was just returning from a hunt when he saw the girl and felt pity. Gently, his men carried her into the palace and lay her on a soft mat.

When she awoke, she was bathed and dressed in a rich robe. The prince was amazed at her beauty and as the two spent time together, he decided that she should be his wife.

"But my son, we don't know who she is," said the king. "How can you marry just like that?" Yet the prince begged and pleaded until at last his parents agreed.

After the grand wedding, the two lived in comfort and contentment. Until one day, when suddenly the wife laughed, thinking of that long ago piece of meat and how her life had changed.

"What is funny?" asked the prince and she replied at once, "Your beard reminds me of my father's broom."

As a frown spread across his face, the princess quickly said, "Because it is made of gold and pearls." The prince smiled again, but after that grew very curious about his wife's rich father. He began to question her daily and wanted to meet him. So she grew very upset.

Then her clever dog barked and said, "Don't worry. I can help. I've just heard of a rich man who died. And he had a daughter that he'd never seen. You go be that daughter!"

Overjoyed, the princess went to the rich man's house. She introduced herself as the long lost daughter and was welcomed with great joy. Soon after that, she brought her husband to visit and he saw the great wealth there. He even saw a broom made of gold and pearls. All was well again.

Several months passed and then the dog wanted to test her friendship. He pretended to grow ill. But the princess didn't seem to care. He looked weaker and weaker, but she just ignored him. When he seemed dead, she told her servants to throw him outside.

Most upset, the dog then told the prince the truth about his wife. The prince, just as angry, ordered her to work as a kitchen servant. Her rich clothes and jewels were taken and she wore rags as she worked in sorrow.

One day, the dog really did get sick. This time, the young woman did care. She nursed him faithfully, she brought water, found soft meat, and petted him fondly. As he grew weaker and weaker, she grew truly sad and sang to him softly. When he died, she put his body gently in her small chest.

The prince knew nothing of the dog's death, but he did know that he missed his wife's smile. So at last, he went down to the kitchen and asked her to come back again.

With a smile that now showed true wisdom, she agreed.

"But first," she said, "I must take care of my dear dog's body." When she opened the chest, she stopped in wonder. For the dog's body had turned into gold, and his eyes into two large rubies. Thus, the prince and his wife lived in even greater comfort from that day.

talk about
What is the best gift a friend can give?

Lebanon

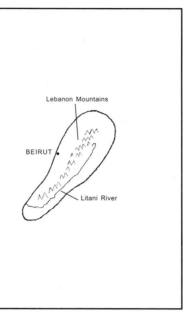

Lebanon, home of the ancient Phoenician civilisation, is a small, mountainous country that became independent from the French in 1943. Its capital, Beirut, was a jewel in West Asia and one of the most cosmopolitan cities in the region. Then, during 1975-1990, a devastating civil war raged, followed in 2006 by the shorter Lebanon War with Israel. Lebanon's mix of cultures and religions give energy to this land, which is rebuilding itself now. Arabic is the official language, but French and English are also spoken by a population that is about 55 per cent Muslim and 40 per cent Christian. The government, too, is balanced: the President should be a Maronite Christian, the Prime Minister a Sunni Muslim, and the Speaker of the National Assembly a Shi'a Muslim. Lebanon's crafts include glassblowing, metalwork, basketry, embroidery, and pottery. Dabkah (the national dance) and *zajal* (folk poetry) are enjoying a revival. Folktales are told, too.

The Patient Wife

ONCE IN LEBANON, there lived a prince with a terrible temper. He would burst into a rage for the slightest reason and everyone feared his cries and tantrums.
So, although his face was a fine one and his family a rich one, no woman wished to marry him.

His mother warned him to control his temper so that he could find a good wife, but he only replied, "I will search, mother. Somewhere, I'll find a woman patient enough for my moods."

So search he did, riding long days in all four directions. But his reputation was too well known, and no woman wanted to live daily with loud words and anger.

Now in the same city lived a very tolerant, kind girl. Her patience had grown as she cared for her four lazy sisters, her rather worthless brother, her sickly father, and her sad-faced mother.

One day, the prince's old nurse, who knew the prince had a kind side, too, decided to help him. She went to the girl's home and begged her to marry the prince.

"Perhaps it could work," thought the girl. "And it might help my family, too." So she agreed to a marriage.

"I'll marry you on one condition," said the prince soon after. "You must stay, by yourself, in a house in the woods, without books or friends. You cannot talk to anyone or do any crafts. You are free to leave at any time, but if you stay for three years, then you'll be my wife."

"I agree," she said. "But you must do two things as well. Bring me a small tree for company, and promise to grant me one wish on our marriage day."

So, a small, healthy tree was placed in the hall of the house in the woods and then the prince left her.

It was a very long three years. But she was a strong young woman and her thoughts were entertaining. She had all of nature, too, to watch and enjoy.
The river, the trees, the birds, and small animals – all made her smile. Every day, she spoke to the tree as well, pouring out her loneliness and any complaints she had. Fortunately, she had often heard her father recite the Qur'an, so she was able to recite those sacred words daily to bring peace. Thus passed three years.

"I am amazed at how you stayed so well," said the prince when he returned at last. "But why did you want that tree?"

Without waiting for her reply, he picked it up to throw it away. But suddenly, it collapsed, as if rotten.

"What happened to it?" he asked. "When I cut that, it was a fine, healthy tree."

"Dear prince," she said. "Nothing can grow or survive well if words of complaint or anger are always put on it. The poor tree heard my lonely words and complaints for three long years and thus it is now destroyed."

He looked at her, with a new respect in his eyes as he thought of her words. Quickly, the arrangements for the marriage were made and the two were wed. But on the wedding night, she made him swear before his parents that he would grant her wish. After he agreed, she said, "All you must do is this. Whenever you feel yourself growing angry and ready to lose your temper, you must go into a room alone, and stay for half an hour. I stayed alone for three years, so surely you can manage that short a time. Then you may come out."

The prince almost laughed at the strange and simple request but he agreed. After that, whenever he felt a rage coming, he stepped into the room. When half an hour had passed, his anger had as well. He came out quiet and thoughtful.

Soon, his temper had cooled, and whenever he grew really angry, he thought first of the results. He began to use more wisdom and patience himself, and was most grateful to his wise, kind wife. The two were soon the best examples of the Prophet's wisdom: "A strong person is not the person who throws his enemies to the ground. A strong person is the one who contains himself when he is angry."

Oman

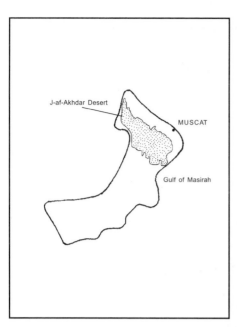

Once known for a rich incense trade, magnificent forts, and the fabled city of Ubar, Oman struggled through long hard years, too. It lost its pearl business to Japan, then its beautiful sailing ships, the *dhows*, suffered losses as steamships arrived. By 1970, when Sultan Qaboos began to rule, the small nation was very backward economically, with just one school and ten km of paved roads. Today, it has world-class hospitals, highways, wealth, and a fine educational system. A vast desert plain covers most of central Oman, with mountains and hills in the north and south, and a 1700-km coastline along the Gulf of Oman and the Arabian Sea. More than half of Oman's population is Arab and the official language is Arabic, but large numbers of South Asians work there as well. Oman's traditional crafts include metal works, woodcarving, weaving, ship building, and pottery. And stories like this are passed on, too.

The Pious Cat

ONE DAY, a cat sat outside in the courtyard to warm himself. Suddenly he heard a sound and looked up. A rat was running along the edge of the roof.

"O Allah our Protector, preserve him!" said the cat.

"May Allah preserve nobody!" snapped the rat, annoyed. "Don't worry about me, just leave me alone!"

Just then the rat tripped over a waterspout and fell to the ground. There, the cat caught him firmly in his claws and purred, "When I called on Allah, you grew angry and said wrong words. Now you see what happens because of that!"

"Ah, you are wise indeed, Uncle Cat," said the rat. "Please give me a chance for forgiveness. Let me pray before I die."

The cat stared hungrily at the rat and thought for a moment.

"I know," said the rat, "you could pray with me to ask for the ending I deserve."

Nodding his head slowly, the cat agreed. He raised his paws in the attitude of prayer, and let go of the rat. At once, the rat scampered to the safety of his hole. Tricked and hungry, the cat rubbed its face sadly, sighing for the lost meal.

So whenever you see a cat today rubbing his face, you'll know he is remembering the delicious smell of a rat.

Palestine

The land of Palestine, once so green and pleasant, has seen war for too long. Occupation by Israelis has shaped a people who remain proud and resistant and yet are dependent upon Israel – since goods need to be exported there and many Palestinians work there. In 1988, a historic declaration of an independent Republic of Palestine (made of the Northern District and the Gaza District) was made by Yasser Arafat, the leader of the Palestine Liberation Organisation (founded in 1964); about 100 nations recognise it today. The culture of Palestine, with its exquisite embroidery, its folk dance, literature, and so much more, has suffered along with its people. Ramzy and Suzy Baroud share a glimpse of the great loss in that land.

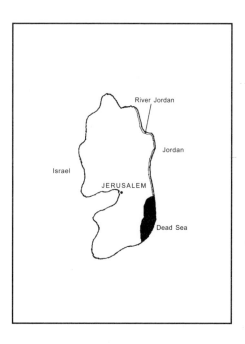

My Mother, Palestine

(MY MOTHER) CAME INTO THE WORLD in the peaceful and green village of Beit Daras. Her first five years there were happy. Hers was a small village adorned with lush green fields, olive groves, and acres of fragrant lemon and orange trees. The landscape was beautiful and the atmosphere was permeated with a sense of simplicity and stillness.

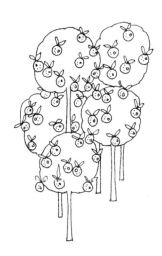

Then the Zionists came. They invaded her village and drove everyone out at gunpoint. My grandmother recalls how the villagers gathered together and fearfully plotted their retaliation against the invaders. The Zionists were armed with weapons provided by the departing British, while the people of my mother's village had only simple farming and kitchen tools to fight with. (Many died in the fight for the village and, the rest fled to refugee camps in the Gaza Strip).

Now my mother (at five) was a refugee. For the rest of her life she would live in a lowly camp, riddled with disease, surrounded by barbed wire, filled with despair. Here she would grow up, marry, become a mother. (Years later, she married a neighbour's son.)

When they married, they had nothing but each other. For years they survived on soup my mother created from discarded garlic skins, grass, and salt. Soon after they were married they had a son, Anwar. He was their shining pride. They adored him. He was their only son and he brought a rare joy to their lives. Anwar was two years old when he became very sick. My mother and father tried to take him to a hospital, but the refugee hospitals had little or no resources to provide for the masses of people. My mother carried Anwar on her back for miles to a makeshift clinic established by the UN. Her hope was lost when all they had to offer her was two aspirin tablets.

Quietly, she took them and walked home with her dying son on her back. She did everything she could to make him comfortable. And she wept and sat beside him as he died. My father was completely filled with despair and rage.

Even today he is overcome with grief at the mention of Anwar's name.

Time passed and they started to rebuild their family, and had six children. I have beautiful memories of lying under the fig tree in our house reading *Treasure Island* while my mother sat beside me making bread. The smell of fresh bread, the warmth of the sun, and her presence always filled me with calm, even while there was a war outside our door.

We never had money. We lived on bread and canned tomatoes provided by the US. But whenever I wanted a book, my mother somehow found a few lira ... to buy one for me. She couldn't even write her own name. And yet she was the wisest creature I have ever known. Her name was Zarefah, which in Arabic means "unequalled". Her name personified her absolutely...

One night the whole camp was awakened by the soldiers' loudspeakers. I lay frozen and afraid to breathe, listening to their chilling cries. "Every man between the ages of fourteen to sixty is to report to the boys' high school immediately. We will be doing random searches of your houses. If we find anyone hiding at home, he will be shot on the spot."

My mother jumped from her mattress and frantically prepared our clothes as she recited verses from the Qur'an. "Allah is Merciful and Compassionate," she uttered as she put out her five sons' clothes, her face ashen with terror.

With our fathers and our neighbours we made our way through the dark paths of Nuseirat camp. I walked with my friends, wondering what our destiny would be. Some of us thought it was real trouble. Shady, my next door neighbour, thought we were going to receive an award. I jokingly hit his arm and laughed nervously at the suggestion.

We arrived at the school to meet up with more than 20,000 other men. The school was surrounded with jeeps and tanks. There were soldiers everywhere. Their floodlights lit up the school grounds. We spent the entire night there while the soldiers systematically grabbed a young boy here, a man there, striking their arms with wooden clubs and pounding their legs with heavy blows. Many were chosen as examples of what happens to "terrorist stone-throwers." It was the longest, most horrifying night of my life. I will never forget it. I do not want to forget it.

At dawn we were released. Of the mass assembly, at least half returned home with a fractured arm or leg.

The nightmare didn't stop that night.

It was early in the morning when they came to our house. We sat on the floor with our pajamas on. My mother had boiled tea and we were having a breakfast of tea, bread, and eggs. A thundering noise came from the door. It was broken down and dozens of soldiers poured into our house. As my father tried to reason with them and my mother screamed and cried, they dragged me and my four brothers out to the street. While we were still in our pajamas, they tied our arms and legs together. My father came and diplomatically, yet frantically, tried to convince the soldiers to let us go. Their leader yelled, "We'll show you what happens to boys who don't follow the rules."

As they were about to strike us with their clubs, my mother, in a frenzy, ran at them. She cried, *"Allahu Akbar"* (God is Greater) and made herself a human barricade between her sons and the soldiers.

One soldier took his gun and thrust it into my mother. It was not a bayonet, but it penetrated into her chest like a dull sword. She gasped and fell to the ground. My father screamed. My brothers began to cry. We couldn't do anything because we were tied up.

The soldiers backed away and my father ran to my mother's side, waiting. He held her head and kissed her hands as the blood trickled out of her mouth. It took fifty days until she finally died. My father did not leave her side for one moment. He sat holding her hands and kissing her feet until the last. As I remember her now, the only comfort I have is that on the fiftieth day her frail body was swiftly swept up into the arms of Allah.

My mother fought and died to defend her children. Until we are free, we will not cease in our struggle. Our mother, Palestine, will one day be liberated. This I am sure is true.

talk about

Who is a refugee? Why are there so many refugees in the world?

Qatar

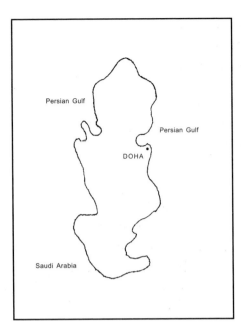

Qatar, a small peninsula known earlier for its pearl diving, received its independence from Great Britain in 1971. Its oil and natural gas reserves have given it one of the highest per capita incomes in the world. Qatar is an absolute monarchy where immigrants outnumber native Qataris. Bedouin nomads from the central part of the Arabian Peninsula were the first settlers; today's residents are largely Sunni Muslims, with Arabic the official language. Dar al-Kutub al-Qatariyya, established in 1962, is one of the oldest national libraries in the Gulf and the Arab world. Perhaps this tale is in a book there, for it is a popular version of a Cinderella-type story, starring a fisherman's kind daughter.

The Fisherman's Daughter

ONCE ON THE SHORES of Qatar, there lived a poor fisherman. He and his wife had a daughter with eyes like dark pearls and she was their wealth. Then one terrible day, the wife suddenly grew ill and died, leaving the two alone and lost in sorrow. Many tears and several years passed. But as the girl grew up, her father only seemed to grow more sad and lonely.

"Father," she said one day, "it is time for you to find another wife."

At first he refused, for he worried that a second wife might not be kind to his daughter. But the girl gently urged him again and again So at last he married a neighbour, and after some time they, too, had a girl.

All too soon, the new mother began to favour her own child and to ill-treat the first daughter. The poor girl had to do all the dirtiest work, such as cleaning the fish, and was never given enough to eat. Her dear father was away fishing all the time, so he never realised her pain.

One day, the mother called the girl and gave her five small fish to clean by the shore, then cut for dinner. After the girl had cut four fish, the last one suddenly spoke, "Please don't kill me. Throw me back in the water instead and I promise to help you."

The kind girl threw the fish in at once, and walked home with a smile. But the mother was furious when she saw one fish gone. She didn't feed the girl, she simply sent her out of the house. Hungry and sad, the girl ran back to the sea. There she saw a fine silver platter covered with the best Qatari butter and the softest crab. She ate happily and thanked her new friend, the small fish.

Days after that, a big drumming party was announced at the home of the shaikh. Everyone quickly dressed in their best and set off. Everyone but the girl.

"You can't go," said her stepmother. "You're too dirty and you have work here to do." Soon the girl, left all alone, ran crying to the shore. But there on the sand was a richly embroidered robe and sparkling diamond sandals. With a great smile and a wave to the fish, the girl dressed and joined the party.

She shone brighter than a desert sun as she sang and laughed. The shaikh could look only at her. All of a sudden, when the party was almost over, she raced quickly home, changed back to her rags, and went to sleep. But she ran so fast that one of her sandals fell off and down the well.

The shaikh and his friends searched for her, following her into the night. And although they didn't find her, they did see something shining in the well, and the shaikh happily took the sandal home.

The next morning, he went from house to house seeking the owner of the sandal. When he came to the fisherman's home, the stepmother hid the first girl in their stone oven and pushed her own child to the bed, where she sat to try on the sandal. Of course it didn't fit and the shaikh turned sadly away when suddenly the cock crowed and called, "My ugly aunt is on the bed and my beautiful aunt is in the oven."

As the cock continued to crow, the shaikh and his men found the right girl. She slipped her foot easily into the sandal and soon after, the two were married in the grandest wedding. The bride ran to the sea to bid farewell to her friend, the fish. And then the lovely couple lived well and in peace for many years. As for the other girl, luck was not her friend.

talk about

Does this story remind you of another story? And another, in another language?

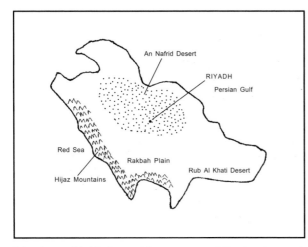

Saudi Arabia

Saudi Arabia, which occupies nearly four-fifths of the Arabian Peninsula, is an absolute monarchy with one of the more conservative Islamic governments in West Asia. Crops in this oil-rich land include dates, wheat, and barley. A rich heritage of poetry and oral literature has been passed on here since the early days of the Bedouins, sharing values of generosity, courage and hospitality. Thousands come on a Hajj pilgrimage to Makkah, the holiest city in the world for Muslims. In 1325, an observant 21-year-old named Ibn Battuta set out on a pilgrimage there. He later travelled about 1,15,872 km in the Islamic world; his journal is now one of the best records of that 14th century world. The excerpts below are from his time in Makkah.

Ibn Battuta visits Makkah

WE SAW BEFORE OUR EYES the illustrious Ka'aba (may God increase it in veneration), like a bride displayed on the bridal chair of majesty and the proud mantles of beauty...We drank of the water of the well of Zamzam which, if you drink it seeking restoration from illness, God restoreth thee; if you drink it for satiation from hunger, God satisfieth thee; if you drink it to quench thy thirst, God quencheth it...

The citizens of Makkah are given to well-doing, of (great) generosity and good disposition, liberal to the poor, to those who have renounced the world, and kindly toward strangers...When anyone has his bread baked (at a public oven) and takes it away to his house, the destitute follow him and he gives to each one of them, sending none away disappointed. Even if he has but a single loaf, he gives away a third or a half of it, cheerfully and without grudgingness.

Another good habit of theirs is that orphan children make a practice of sitting in the bazaar, each with two baskets, one large and one small. A man of Makkah comes to the bazaar, where he buys grain, meat, and vegetables, and passes these to a boy, who puts the grain in one basket and the meat and vegetables in the other and takes them to the man's house, so that his meal may be prepared. Meanwhile the man goes about his devotions and his business. There is no instance related of any of the boys having ever abused their trust in this matter – on the contrary he delivers what he has been given to carry with the most scrupulous honesty. They receive for this a fixed fee of a few coppers.

The Makkans are elegant and clean in their dress, and as they mostly wear white their garments always appear spotless and snowy. They use perfume freely, paint their eyes with kohl, and are constantly cleaning their teeth with slips of green arak-wood...The people of Makkah eat only once in the day, after the afternoon prayer...If anyone wishes to eat at any other time of day, he eats dried dates, and it is for that reason that their bodies are healthy and that diseases and infirmities are rarely found amongst them.

Syria

Syria, at the eastern end of the Mediterranean Sea, is a land of deserts, plains, and mountains, with the Euphrates its most important river. The ancient city of Damascus, the capital today, was long known for its wise rule. The traveller, Ibn Battuta, wrote of endowments there to aid travellers, provide for marriages, help those on the Hajj, build roads, and even to replace broken vessels. Arabs make up about 90 per cent of the population today (Kurds and Armenians are the largest minorities), Arabic is the official language, and Sunni Islam the predominant religion. Embroidery is an important traditional craft, which is found now in high fashion gowns and jackets, too. The Crusades were fought in this land, and those days come alive in a fascinating journal by a Muslim gentleman and warrior of the time. Here are two small true stories from his journal; the first was an anecdote reported to him.

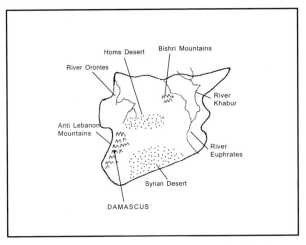

The Diary of an Arab-Syrian Gentleman

I WAS FOND OF HUNTING. So I went out one day to hunt and a group of Franks fell upon me, captured me and shut me up all alone in a dungeon. The master of Bayt-Jibril fixed my ransom at two thousand dinars. I remained in the dungeon a year without anybody inquiring about me.

But one day as I was in my dungeon, behold! the trapdoor was lifted and a Bedouin was lowered towards me. I said, "Where did they take you from?"

"From the road," he replied. After staying with me a few days, his ransom was fixed at fifty dinars. One day he said to me, "Do you know that none can deliver you from this dungeon but me? Deliver me so that I may deliver you."

I said to myself, "Here is a man who, finding himself in distress, seeks for himself a way of deliverance." So I answered not. A few days later he repeated the same request to me. So I said to myself, "By Allah, I will surely make an effort to deliver him, for maybe Allah will deliver me as a reward." So I shouted to the jailer and said, "Tell the lord I wish to talk with him." The jailer went away and returned. Then he took me out of the dungeon and presented me before the lord. I said to the lord, "I have been in your prison for one year without anybody inquiring about me. Nobody knows whether I am alive or dead. You have imprisoned with me this Bedouin and fixed his ransom at fifty dinars. Now, add his ransom to mine and let me send him to my father so that he may buy me off."

"Do so," replied the lord. So I returned and told the Bedouin who went out, bade me farewell and departed.

I awaited results from him for two months, but I saw no trace of him nor heard any news about him. So I lost hope. But one night, to my great surprise, he appeared before me from a tunnel in the side of the dungeon and said, "Arise. By Allah, I have been five months digging this passage from a village in ruins until I got to you."

I stood and we went out through that passage. He broke my chain,

It is easier to make a camel jump a ditch than to make a fool listen to reason.
— *a Kurdish saying*

133

accompanied me to my own home. And now I know not what to admire more —
his faithfulness in carrying out his promise or his precision in digging a tunnel that
exactly hit the side of the dungeon.

...We looked down from a rugged hill overlooking all the lowland below, and saw a
lion lying on the bank of a river right beneath the hill. So we stopped in our place,
not daring to descend for fear of the beast. Presently we saw a man advancing.
We called loudly to him and waved our clothes to him in order to warn him against
the lion, but he did not stop. He tightened his bowstring, fixed an arrow in it and
marched along. The lion saw him and sprang toward him, but the man instantly
shot his arrow, which did not miss the heart of the lion, and killed it.

Then the man took his arrow and came to the river. He removed his shoes,
took off his clothes and went down to bathe in the water. Then he went up and put
on his clothes — while we were still looking at him — and he began to shake his hair
in order to dry it from the water. After that he put on one shoe and leaned upon his
side and remained leaning for a long time. We said to ourselves, "By Allah, he did
very well, but why is he showing off?"

We went to him while he was still in the same position and found him
dead. We could not tell what killed him. Then we took off the shoe from his foot
and, behold! A small scorpion that was in it had bitten him in his big toe, and he
died on the spot. So we were amazed at this case of this hero who killed a lion, but
was killed by a scorpion as big as a finger. How mysterious, therefore, are the works
of Allah, the Almighty.

talk about
Keeping a diary.

Turkey

Mustafa Kemal, the 'Father of the Turks', founded modern Turkey in 1923 in a land that once contained one of the world's earliest civilisations. Turkey, eager to join the European Union, has long been a bridge between the East and the West. Traders and scholars have crossed its lands for centuries and, from a base in Constantinople (now Istanbul), the grand Ottoman Empire once stretched from Budapest to Baghdad. The great Suleiman ruled the empire at its height, in the 16th century, and left behind a legacy of architectural beauty and justice. Turkish music and literature also draw from a rich mixture, and in 2006, novelist Orhan Pamuk became the first Turkish person to receive a Nobel Prize. Kurds, eager for independence, make up about 2 per cent of the population. The majority of the population is Muslim, and the official language is Turkish, a language that shares the wit and wisdom of the popular Hoja.

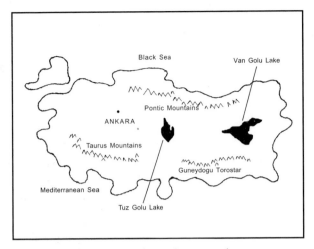

The Wit of Nasruddin Hoja

WHAT IS MY TRUE WORTH, my value?" demanded the great warrior Timur of Nasruddin Hoja. "You see before you a man who has conquered the whole world, who has slain armies and makes the mountains tremble! Look carefully and tell me what you think is my real worth." The Hoja peered at the emperor, stroked his chin and replied, "About 20 gold pieces."

"What? Idiot!" raged Timur. "My belt alone is worth 20 gold pieces!"

The Hoja nodded. "I included that when I gave you my estimate," he said.

Another time, Nasruddin Hoja and his travelling companion were destitute. Pooling their last *paras*, they had just enough money to buy a single glass of milk at an inn. "You drink your half first, Hoja," said the friend. "I have a little sugar in my pocket, and I want to stir it into my half of the milk."

"Well, stir it in," said the Hoja. "Sweetened milk would be a grand treat!"

"No, you drink your half first," the friend insisted. "I only have enough sugar for my half."

"Well, in that case," grumbled Nasreddin Hoja, reaching for the salt-cellar, "I think I'll drink my half salty."

Another day, Nasruddin Hoja was standing in a field when a passerby quizzed him, asking what the people in the next village down the road were like. "Well, what did you think of the people in our village?" he asked the stranger. "Block-headed, lazy, stupid and rude," replied the traveller.

"That's probably how you'll find them in the next village, too," said the Hoja.

A little later, another passing stranger struck up a conversation with Nasruddin Hoja. He too asked what the people in the next village were like. "How did you find the people in this village?" countered the Hoja again. "Warm-hearted, smiling, gentle and hospitable," answered the stranger. "Then that's how you'll find them in the next village, too."

Children pour water on the street, their parents slip and fall in it.
– *a Turkish saying*

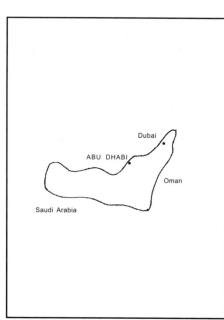

UAE

The United Arab Emirates has desert land covering over 90 per cent of the country, with rich oases and grand dunes, along with mountains in the east. Comprised of seven autonomous emirates, the UAE is now one of the richest nations in the world. Under the wise leadership of Sheikh Zayed, the UAE has also developed into one of the world's most generous foreign aid donors. It provides free health care, financial assistance for weddings, and a fine education to its citizens. The official language is Arabic although a number of languages are spoken among the large expatriate community. Both camel and horse racing are favourite sports there, while falconry has been long been popular, from earlier days when this type of hunting helped to supplement the diet. Dubai city is growing as a centre for regional film, television, and music production. It is indeed difficult to picture the hard life shown in the beginning of this small teaching tale from the UAE.

The Hen

ONE YEAR THERE WAS even less water than usual in the desert. The rain didn't fall and everything dried up. All the birds had a terrible time and wondered what to do. There was so little to eat and nothing to drink.

At last, the birds came together to think of a solution.

Every bird in the country came, all colours were there, all sizes, too. And all were very unhappy.

As they squawked and crowed and cried at once, it took a while to share any idea. But after hours of meeting, they all agreed on a plan. They would fly together to a new home, one with more shady trees and rich grass and plentiful water.

So all the crows said, "Tomorrow, Inshallah (if Allah wills), we'll fly to a new and better home."

All the pheasants said, ""Tomorrow, Inshallah, we'll fly to a new and better home."

All the falcons and hawks and so many others agreed, "Tomorrow, Inshallah, we'll fly to a new and better home."

Only the hens kept quiet.

The next day, all the birds except for the hens found that they could fly high and soar far to a new and pleasant land. But the hens could not fly away. The hens could not fly at all. They could not move to a new and pleasant land. The hens had to stay. And so it is said, that hens still cannot fly today because they alone did not admit Allah's power.

Yemen

South Yemen became the Arab world's only Marxist nation after independence from Britain, but war with North Yemen continued until 1990, when the two merged to become the United Republic of Yemen. The landscape is varied, with four main regions: coastal plains in the west, highlands to the east and west, and part of the Great Sandy Desert in the east. This rugged country, known for its coffee, has no oil wealth and is struggling to raise its low literacy rates and per capita income. Yet its history includes the inspiring reigns of several strong queens (including the legendary Queen of Sheba) and the riches of the early incense trade in myrrh and frankincense. This tale, collected and written by Carolyn Han while she studied in Yemen, speaks of wealth, too, and of waste, as it shares the story of a local landmark.

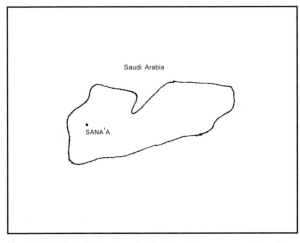

The Wedding Cakes

SADDLE THE CAMEL," Muhammad ordered the men. The camel complained loudly as they placed an elegant red rug on its back and then strapped on the leather saddle. Muhammad and his men had been hired as the bridal escort for the women's wedding party.

"A wedding to remember," the wealthy villagers said. "We'll spare no expense."

A woman dressed in fine velvet opened the wooden shutters and shouted, "Ya Muhammad, make sure that the cakes are on the ground."

"Yes, Sayyida," he replied in a most respectful voice. Muhammad told his men to pack the freshly baked cakes into sacks and load them on a donkey.

"Stay in front of the procession and place the cakes along the road," he said. "The camel has to step on them as he carries the bride to Rada."

"All the way to Rada?" the men asked. "It will take hundreds of cakes."

"That's true," Muhammad said, shrugging his shoulders.

"Why don't they eat the cakes?" the men protested. "These cakes could feed the poor villagers." Each time a man placed a cake on the ground, he thought of another hungry person.

Wearing a colourful wedding costume and long flowing veil, the bride perched on top of the camel's saddle. Her brother snapped his fingers, which was the cue for Muhammad to release the rope that was tied around the camel's left front leg. When Muhammad loosened the rope, the bride first pitched backward and then forward as the camel stood. With shouts of joy – tongue-trilling from the crowd – the bride balanced securely and the procession moved forward.

More than a hundred women – dressed in shimmering brocade gowns, flowing scarves, heavy silver bracelets and anklets and row upon row of silver necklaces – took part in the wedding celebration. They seemed not to notice the poor villagers dressed in rags watching from the sidelines.

"Stop the camel!" the bride's brother shouted, "It's not stepping on the cakes."

"The camel has only missed a few," Muhammad replied.

"It must crush them all," the brother yelled. Hungry onlookers standing along the road watched the cakes smash under the camel's big padded feet.

Before reaching Rada, the wedding party had to cross a wide *wadi*, a dry riverbed.

"The camel missed some cakes," the brother shouted. "Turn back!"

Muhammad tugged at the camel's lead rope, but it would not budge. He pulled again and again. When he looked back, the camel, bride, and wedding procession had turned into a sculpted mountain of sandstone.

Although the lead rope has long disappeared, the worn stone figures near Ras al-Ga are still visible today – they stand as a reminder of what can happen when people flaunt their wealth by wasting food.

talk about
Why so many
go hungry.

VISUAL ARTS

ROUNDABOUTS IN OMAN

The city of Muscat in Oman is known for its many and interesting traffic roundabouts. Each centre has a large object to capture attention: a huge frankincense burner, a jug with delicate metalwork pouring coffee into cups, high domes with blue and gold tiles, a large thatched hut, and more. Students can work in groups to create some of their own traffic circle art!

Materials

Materials gathered by students: scrap, natural materials, clay, little toys

Method

❖ Tell students about the traffic circles. Explain that they will be creating their own original roundabouts.
❖ Divide them into groups of five. Have them brainstorm ideas then gather needed materials as homework.
❖ With chalk, draw a circle (or have students draw) on the floor/ground, with a diameter of about one metre.
❖ Have each group then create a big object or a scene for their circles.
❖ After they are done, everyone can walk around and enjoy the traffic art.

Note: Smaller circles could be made, with a road weaving around them, then actual homemade or store bought vehicles could 'drive' around them for fun.

DOORS OF SAUDI ARABIA

In Saudi Arabia, as in other parts of West Asia, decorated doors are an important part of a house. The house itself might look plain on the outside, with unbroken walls to keep out the heat and to help the family look into itself, and perhaps a courtyard. But the doors would be welcoming: many with varied, elegant geometric designs; some in patterns of blues, reds, and yellows; some brown with lacy white decorations; others in broad bands of colors or carved from fine wood. Students can have fun designing their own doors.

Materials

Drawing surface: chalkboard, ground, paper
Colours for surface: chalk, markers, coloured pencils, paints
Scissors

Method

❖ Discuss the popularity and variety of the decorated door as mentioned above.
❖ Have students cut or draw an outline of a door. It can be any shape they wish: rectangular, archlike, curved in other ways.
❖ Challenge them to create a very special door, with patterns and colors they choose.
❖ If doors are made from paper, students can attach an inside picture behind door, to be seen when door is opened.

Note: Students can make big doors on the ground instead, as a small group project, decorating with natural objects.

ZOOMORPHIC CALLIGRAPHY

One of the most striking art forms in West Asia and in other Muslim lands, is the art of calligraphy. Not only are there incredible copies of the holy Qur'an, but many objects, from bowls and metalwork to armor and huge buildings, bear a wise saying or a verse from the Qur'an. In one of the most challenging styles, letters or words are combined in the shape of an animal (see here and on next page). Students can enjoy making their own experiments with this intriguing style.

Materials

Sample pictures
Pen and pencil

Method

- ❖ Ask if students have seen examples of calligraphy, in any language.
- ❖ Tell them of one special form of written artistry in Islamic calligraphy: zoomorphic figures, where the letters of the alphabet or a verse or saying is made in the shape of an animal.
- ❖ Show them copies of the examples here.
- ❖ Challenge them to take a simple word in their own alphabet and to form the letters into the shape of an animal or object. Allow enough time to experiment, it is not an easy task.

VERBAL/WRITTEN ARTS

TRAVEL JOURNALS

The journal of Ibn Battuta is famous throughout West Asia. He wrote carefully of life in many countries in Asia during his time, describing mosques and worship, individuals, landscapes, problems, leaders and rulers, food, ways of transportation, and much more. The art of the travel diary is one used often across Asia. Students can write a small part of a travel diary themselves, following his example.

Materials

Pencil and paper

Method

- ❖ Have students read the selection from Ibn Battuta. Discuss the kinds of things he described in these brief sections. Ask if they've read any other travel diaries, or if they have even kept one.
- ❖ Each student then chooses one place he or she has travelled to – from a local market to a far city.

- ❖ Students each write a page of travel comment/ diary, noting clothes, climate, sounds, and more (they can use both true facts and imaginative details they've created).
- ❖ Students read their writing to class, or share in small groups.

Note: The travel journal can also be assigned about one culture you have studied, if you have enough reference material to give students the right details.

READ AND WRITE FOR CHANGE

The very moving piece on Palestine will make students think about a most unjust situation. Help them to further explore the truth there and to work, through the pen and other means, for needed change.

Materials

Pencil and paper
List of ideas to write on board or read

Method

- ❖ Have students read 'My Mother, Palestine'.
- ❖ Discuss the feelings it brought up.
- ❖ Ask them what they know of the situation there.
- ❖ Challenge them to do research on the web or in a library to find out the background and to know both sides of the story.
- ❖ Share the findings and decide if Israel is acting unfairly now.
- ❖ If students agree, after their research, with the need to help Palestine, then share the following suggestions and decide on which tasks – including other ideas – your class can do to help.

Source Material

How to Help the Palestinian Cause
(ideas adapted from www.palestineonlinestore)

- ❖ Spread awareness about the Palestinian issue: After you have the facts about the problem, then teach others. Write about it for your school newspaper.
- ❖ Media lobbying: Make sure that the newspapers give fair, unbiased news about the issues. Write letters to them.

- ❖ Political lobbying: Make sure that your government has a balanced position on the region.
- ❖ Humanitarian aid: If possible, help raise funds for the Palestine Children's Relief Fund, since children are the most hurt by the situation.
- ❖ Display your solidarity: Print the message to free Palestine on cards, posters, displays to show you care.

SONGS/GAMES

AN ARABIC RHYME

Around the world, children still chant rhymes, although as various technologies overwhelm childhood in many areas, these little treasures are in danger. Share this lovely, simple nursery rhyme from Iraq and invite students to share ones they remember.

Materials and Method

Share the rhyme below with children (ask them to share other rhymes they remember).

Coocookti – Little Dove

Coocookti bil Hillah,
Shi tackul? Bajillah.
Sha tishrub? Mai allah.
Wain itiruh? Bab allah.

Little dove from Hila,
What do you eat? *Bajillah* (large bean)
What do you drink? *Mai allah* (God's water)
Where are you going? *Bab allah* (God's door)
(Shabbas: 1979, 7)

SEVEN STONES GAME

Seven stones is a traditional game, somewhat like baseball, played by Arab village children in Palestine in better, happier times (today, the games are often war games, complete with very realistic gunfire sound effects).

Materials

an empty field or playground

a volleyball
seven stones (flat type best)

Method

- ❖ Explain the rules below and play!

Source Material

Object: score runs by knocking down stones with ball, then running around bases before ball is caught and stones are restacked.

Set-up: Large diamond is made on field, with three bases and a home plate. The stones are stacked in a pile near centre, but closer to home plate. Two teams are formed.

Action: One team stands behind stones, while the other takes turns trying to knock down stones, pitching from behind home base. The batter is out if s/he misses three times. If s/he hits stones, s/he runs around bases while the other team tries to restack stones and get ball. As soon as the stones are restacked, the runner can be tagged out by throwing ball at her/him or touching her/him with it. If s/he reaches a base, s/he is safe. If s/he reaches home, it's a home run. Play continues until the team has three outs, then the teams exchange positions and continue. Play can go on as desired, up to any number of innings.

NATURE/SCIENCE

WASTE NOT

The almost satirical description of a frugal landlord/scrap collector, by the clever writer, Al-Jahiz, reminds us all how much can be saved today, as it was then. Many West Asian countries use resources wisely and recycle with great ingenuity. Students can share this knowledge.

Materials

Will depend on format of project

Method

(Note: This project is best open-handed since it explores resourcefulness, so help students decide

how to share their ideas and gather materials themselves.)

❖ After reading the excerpt from Al-Jahiz, discuss the types of waste students have seen or read about by people in their region or elsewhere. Then discuss the types of recycling seen.

❖ Help students to brainstorm and decide on a way to encourage recycling and a resourceful use of materials, working in groups or alone. Consider these types of activities and more:
Letter to newspaper with ideas for recycling
Poster encouraging recycling, with examples drawn
Small drama showing scenes of clever recycling
Art project from recycled materials

❖ Encourage them to plan their projects, find materials as needed, and then proceed.

❖ When all of the projects are finished, arrange for some type of sharing: performances, a show and tell, informal reports, etc.

ENGINEERING INGENUITY

Many advances in science came about in West Asia; Islamic cultures led the world for years in such discoveries. To this day, many of the clever, resourceful ways to conserve and use water in West Asia remain unknown outside the region. And a very interesting book that shares some fascinating engineering inventions, *The Book of Ingenious Devices* (see biblio for details, p. 144), should also be better known. One invention is shared below so that students can try their hand at a similar device.

Materials

A large copy of the drawing below – on chalk board or large paper – to illustrate device
Papers and pencils
Description below to read

Method

❖ Show the students the ingenious device. Introduce the title of the book and explain that it had a number of clever devices for pouring water, for oil burning lamps, and more.

❖ Read the description below to show how this device worked.

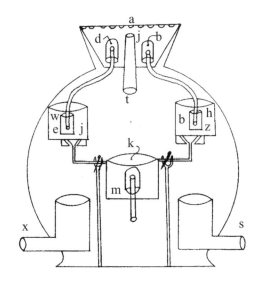

❖ As a class, discuss and list similar inventions that could be designed to help with a simple task.

❖ Have students choose one idea, or use their own, and sketch out a device – even it isn't too practical – that could do the job. The device should be drawn as a diagram, with notes and explanations written as needed.

❖ Have fun sharing ideas and if one actually seems like it could work, consider making and selling it!!!

Source Material

This invention helps you to do a "magic" trick. As people watch, a mixture of wine and water is poured into a big jar. Yet, when liquid comes out of the bottom of the jar, wine comes out on one side and water from the other. How is it done?

❖ First, without anybody watching, pour water into the top of the jar carefully, into pipe BZ and into tank HZ.

❖ Then pour wine into the top on the other side. It goes into pipe DE and into tank EW.
Now, in front of people who are watching, mix wine and water and pour the mixture into the centre of jar top. It goes down pipe JT and into tank KM.

❖ That tank gets heavy and sinks.

❖ When it does, it makes valves B and J open, and suddenly water flows down and then comes out from outlet S and the same happens to wine, which flows out of outlet X.
(Hill: 1979,168)

THINGS TO THINK ABOUT

TOO MUCH SHOW

In 'The Wedding Cakes' from Yemen, the problems of inequality and of ostentatious spending/display are shared. These are problems that continue in various parts of Asia, especially in countries with a wide gap between rich and poor. Some governments are trying to attack the problem: in Pakistan, the law now prohibits ostentatious displays and wasteful expenses for marriages. Students can educate others about this important issue of equality.

Materials

Large sheets of paper
Colours of some type: markers, paints

Methods

❖ After reading 'The Wedding Cakes', discuss the problem of such showy spending. Find examples from local and national newspapers or stories.

❖ Brainstorm how to avoid such displays and the inequalities behind them: promoting simpler lifestyles, encouraging more fair distribution of wealth, increasing awareness, passing laws, etc.

❖ Have students, with partners, design a poster to educate others: illustrate the problem, offer a solution, ask a question, and more.

❖ Remind them that posters are usually bold and bright, to attract attention.

❖ Display the posters in a public space so that adults in the community can also think about the problem.

PATIENT ADVICE

In 'The Patient Wife', the wife shows great patience and wisdom. As the strongest member in her own family, and as a clever new wife, she learned many things. Pretend that she is offering advice to others on various problems.

Materials

Typical problems from school/home/ neighbourhood (written down on slips of paper): someone bullying or stealing, an unfair teacher, someone lying, etc.

Method

❖ Review the story and talk about the quiet wisdom that the girl showed, how she solved problems – her husband's temper, her loneliness – in simple but clever ways.

❖ Choose a student 'to complain'. Give her a slip with a problem.

❖ Have the student share the problem to class, giving made-up but realistic details. Then class can suggest some ways to deal with it wisely, as the patient wife did.

❖ Continue with another problem and another. This can also be a written activity, with each student writing down his/her advice.

Bibliography

Aghaie, Kamran Scot. *Muslim Women Through the Centuries.* Fountain Valley, CA.:Council on Islamic Education, 1998.

Alavi, Nasrin. *We are Iran: The Persian Blogs.* N.Y.:Soft Skull Press, 2005.

'Attar, Farid al-Din. *Muslim Saints and Mystics.* Chicago: University of Chicago Press, 1966.

Aziz, Barbara Nimri. "The Last Hakawati" *Saudi Aramco World.* J/F 1996,12-17.

Badalkhan, Sabir. "Balochi Oral Tradition." *Oral Tradition.* 18:2, 2003, p. 229-235.

Beck, Brenda, et al, eds. *Folktales of India.* Chicago: University of Chicago Press, 1987.

Bloom, Jonathan and Sheila Blair. *Islam: Empire of Faith.* London: BBC, 2001.

Bordahl, Vibeke. *Chinese Storytellers.* Boston: Cheng & Tsui, 2002.

Bowen, Kevin and Nguyen Ba Chung, trans. *Distant Road: Selected Poems of Nguyen Duy.* Willimantic, CT: Curbstone Press, 1999.

Bushnaq, Inea, trans. *Arab Folktales.* New York: Pantheon Books, 1986.

Carrison, Muriel Paskin. *Cambodian Folk Stories.* Rutland, VT: Charles E. Tuttle, 1987.

Chadwick, Nora and Victor Zhirmunsky. *Oral Epics of Central Asia.Vol.1,2,3.* London: Cambridge University Press, 1969.

Chan, Victor and His Holiness the Dalai Lama. *The Wisdom of Forgiveness.* N.Y.: Riverhead Books, 2004.

Chang, Henry, ed. *Six Insides from the Korean War.* Seoul; Dae-Dong Moon Hwa Sa, 1958.

Choden, Kunzang. *Folktales of Bhutan.* Bangkok: White Lotus, 1993.

Chun Shin-yong, ed. *Korean Folk Tales.* Seoul: Si-sa-yong-o-sa. 1982.

Cirtautus, Ilse. *Folktales Along The Silk Road.* Seattle: University of Washington, 1998.

Clayton, Sally Pomme. *Tales Told in Tents: Stories from Central Asia.* London: Frances Lincoln, 2004.

Cowell, E.B., ed. *The Jataka,* Vol. 1-6. London: Pali Text Society, 1973.

Covington, Richard. "Masterpieces to Go." *Saudi Aramco World.* March/April, 2005, 8-17.

Derks, Will. *The Feast of Storytelling.* Jakarta: RUL, 1994.

Dhar, Asha. *Folk Tales of Afghanistan.* New Delhi: Sterling, 1982.

Dorson, Richard, general ed. *Folktales Told around the World* Series. Chicago: University of Chicago Press.

Eberhardt, Wolfram, ed. *Folktales of China.* New York: Washington Square Press, 1973.

Eigeland, Tor. "The Academy of the Rain Forest" in *Saudi Aramco World.* November/December, 1992, 2 – 11.

El-Shamy, Hasan M. *Tales Arab Women Tell.* Bloomington: Indiana University Press, 1999.

Gibb, H.A.R. *The Travels Of Ibn Battuta.* Cambridge: University Press, 1958.

Ginsburg, Mirra. *The Kaha Bird.* New York: Crown Publishers, 1971.

Gurumurthy, Preemila. *Kathakalaksepa.* Madras: International Society for the Investigation of Ancient Civilizations, 1994.

Ha, Tae-Hung. *Korean Nights Entertainment.* Seoul: Yonsei University, 1969.

Han, Carolyn. *From the Land of Sheba: Yemeni Folk Tales.* Northhampton, MA: Interlink Books, 2005.

Han, Suzanne Crowder. *Korean Folk and Fairy Tales.* Elizabeth: Hollym, 1991.

Hansen, Eric. "The Water Village of Brunei." *Saudi Aramco World.* May/June 1995, 32-39.

Hill, Donald, trans. *The Book of Ingenious Devices by the Banu Musa bin Shakir.* London: D.Reidel, 1979.

Holliday, Laurel. *Children of Israel, Children of Palestine.* N.Y.: Pocket Books, 1998.

Hourani, Albert. *A History of the Arab Peoples.* Cambridge, Mass.: Harvard University Press, 2002.

Htin, Aung U. *Burmese Law Tales: The Legal Element in Burmese Folk-Lore.* London: Oxford University Press, 1962.

Jinzhi, Wei. *One Hundred Allegorical Tales from Traditional Chinese.* Hong Kong: Joint Publishing Company, 1982.

Joseph, Ammu and Kalpana Sharma, ed. *Terror, Counter Terror: Women Speak Out.* London: Zed Books, 2003.

Kershaw, Eva Maria. *Dusun Folktales.* Honolulu: Center for Southeast Asian Studies, 1994.

Khan, Gabriel Mandel. *Arabic Script.* N.Y.: Abbeville Press, 2001.

Koswanage, Niluksi. "Last Tales from a Storyteller." The Sun, 4/28/2002.

Kritzeck, James, ed. *Anthology of Islamic Literature.* New York: New American Library, 1975.

Kupershoek, P. Marcel. *Oral Poetry and Narratives from Central Arabia: The Poetry of ad-Dindan.* Leiden: Brill, 1994.

Lat. *Kampung Boy.* Kuala Lumpur: Berita, 2003.

Mair, Victor H. *Painting and Performance.* Honolulu: University of Hawaii Press, 1988.

Mantin, Peter and Ruth. *The Islamic World*. Cambridge: Cambridge University Press, 1993.

May, Walter. *Manas. The Great Campaign: Kirghiz Heroic Epics*. Traditional Cultures and Environments, 1999.

Mayer, Fanny Hagin, ed. *Ancient Tales in Modern Japan*. Indiana Bloomington University Press, 1984.

——*The Yanagita Kunio Guide to the Japanese Folk Tale*. Indiana University Press, 1986.

Morioka, Heinz and Miyoko Sasaki. *Rakugo, The Popular Narrative Art of Japan*. Cambridge: Council on East Asian Studies at Harvard, 1990.

Muhawi, Ibrahim and Sharif Kanaana. *Speak Bird, Speak Again: Palestinian Arab Folktales*. Berkeley: University of CA Press, 1989.

Munif, Abd Al-Rahman. *Story of a City: A Childhood in Amman*. London: Quartet Books, 1998.

Nicholson, Reynold. *Translations of Eastern Poetry and Prose*. London: Curzon Press, 1987.

Nigel, Phillips. " A note on the relationship between singer and audience in West Sumatran story-telling," *Indonesia Circle*, No. 58, June 1992.

Noonan, John. "Tales of the Hoja." *Saudi Aramco World*. September/October, 1997, p. 30-39.

Nuwayhid, Jamal Salim. *Abu Jameel's Daughter and Other Stories: Arab Folk Tales from Palestine and Lebanon*. Northhampton, MA: Interlink Books, 2002.

Omidsalar, Mahmoud and Teresa. "Narrating Epics in Iran" in *Traditional Storytelling Today* by Margaret Read MacDonald. Chicago: Fitzroy Dearborn, 1999, p. 326-340.

Osman, Mohammed Taib. "The Tradition of Storytelling in Malaysia" in *Traditional Storytelling Today* by Margaret Read MacDonald. Chicago: Fitzroy Dearborn, 1999, p. 138-141.

Park, Chan E. *Voices From the Straw Mat*. Honolulu: University of Hawaii Press, 2003.

Pax, Salam. *Salam Pax: The Clandestine Diary of an Ordinary Iraqi*. N.Y.: Grove Press, 2003.

Pellat, Charles. *The Life and Works of Jahiz*. Berkeley: University of California Press, 1969.

Pellowski, Anne. *The World of Storytelling*. N.Y.: H. W. Wilson, 1990.

Phillipps, Nigel. *Sijobang, Sung Narrative Poetry of West Sumatra*. Cambridge: Cambridge University Press, 1981.

Picard, Barbara Leonie. *Tales of Ancient Persia, Retold from the Shah-Nama of Firdausi*. New York: H. Z. Walck, 1973.

Ramanujan, A.K. *Folktales of India*. N.Y.: Pantheon, 1991.

Ratnapala, Nandasena. *Folklore of Sri Lanka*. Colombo: State Printing Corporation, 1991.

Riordan, James. *Tales from Tartary*. New York: Viking Press, 1978.

Riverbend. *Baghdad Burning: Girl Blog from Iraq*. N.Y.: The Feminist Press, 2005.

Robinson, Francis. *The Cambridge Illustrated History of the Islamic World*. New York: Cambridge University Press, 1998.

Said, Edward. *Orientalism*. New York: Vintage Books, 1994.

Schimmel, Annemarie. *Calligraphy and Islamic Culture*. N. Y.: New York University Press, 1984.

Sen Gupta, Sankar. *The Patas and the Patuas of Bengal*. Calcutta: Indian Publications, 1973.

Senaveratne, John. *Dictionary of Proverbs of the Sinhalese*. Colombo: Times of Ceylon Company, 1936.

Shabbas, Audrey. "The Child in the Arab Family." *The Link*. 12:2, May-June, 1979.

Shaikh, Munir. *Teaching About Islam and Muslims*. Fountain Valley, CA: Council on Islamic Education, 1995.

Shepard, Katya. *The Sandal-Wood Box*. Richard Sadler, 1972.

Spagnoli, Cathy. *Asian Tales and Tellers*. Little Rock: August House, 1998.

Stevens, Catherine. "Peking Drumsinging." Ph.D. Diss., Harvard University, 1972.

Sweeney, Amin. *Malay Word Music*. Dewan Bahasa dan Pustaka, 1994.

Thakuru, Hassan. "We say, 'Enough is Enough' ". khttp://www.dhivehiobserver.com/columns/Hassan_Thakuru/HT6-071220051.htm 7 December 2005

The Sayings of Muhammad. New Delhi: Goodword Books, 1997.

Usmah ibn Munqidh. *An Arab Syrian Gentleman and Warrior in the Period of the Crusades*. Philip K. Hitti, trans. Princeton, N.J.: Princeton University Press, 1987.

Walker, Warren S. & Ahmet E. Uysal. *Tales Alive in Turkey*. Cambridge: Harvard University Press, 1966.

Winner, Thomas. *The Oral Art and Literature of the Kazakhs of Russian Central Asia*. New York: Arno Press, 1980.

Wood, Frances. *The Silk Road*. Berkeley: University of California Press, 2002.

World Folklore Series from Libraries Unlimited, CO.

Yamamoto, Kumiko. *The Oral Background Of Persian Epics*. Leiden: Brill, 2003.

Zim, Jacob. *My Shalom, My Peace*. Tel Aviv: Sabra Books, 1975.

Zong In-sob. *Folk Tales from Korea*. Elizabeth, N.J.: Hollym, 1982.

Story Sources and Credits

Bushnaq, Inea, trans. *Arab Folktales*. New York: Pantheon Books, 1986.

Choden, Kunzang. *Folktales of Bhutan*. Bangkok: White Lotus, 1993.

Cirtautus, Ilse. *Folktales Along The Silk Road*. Seattle: University of Washington, 1998.

Clayton, Sally Pomme. *Tales Told in Tents: Stories from Central Asia.* London: Frances Lincoln, 2004.

Dhar, Asha. *Folk Tales of Afghanistan*. New Delhi: Sterling, 1982.

El-Shamy, Hasan M. *Tales Arab Women Tell*. Bloomington: Indiana University Press, 1999.

Gibb, H.A.R. *The Travels Of Ibn Battuta*. Cambridge: University Press, 1958.

Han, Carolyn. *From the Land of Sheba: Yemeni Folk Tales*. Northhampton, MA: Interlink Books, 2005.

Hansen, Eric. "The Water Village of Brunei." *Saudi Aramco World*. May/June 1995, 32-39.

Hill, Donald, trans. *The Book of Ingenious Devices by the Banu Musa bin Shakir.* London: D.Reidel, 1979.

Holliday, Laurel. *Children of Israel, Children of Palestine*. N.Y.: Pocket Books, 1998.

Htin, Aung U. *Burmese Law Tales: The Legal Element in Burmese Folk-Lore*. London: Oxford University Press, 1962.

Jinzhi, Wei. *One Hundred Allegorical Tales from Traditional Chinese*. Hong Kong: Joint Publishing Company, 1982.

Kershaw, Eva Maria. *Dusun Folktales*. Honolulu: Center for Southeast Asian Studies, 1994.

Kritzeck, James, ed. *Anthology of Islamic Literature*. New York: New American Library, 1975.

May, Walter. *Manas. The Great Campaign: Kirghiz Heroic Epics*. Traditional Cultures and Environments, 1999.

Muhawi, Ibrahim and Kanaana, Sharif. *Speak Bird, Speak Again: Palestinian Arab Folktales*. Berkeley: University of CA Press, 1989.

Munif, Abd Al-Rahman. *Story of a City: A Childhood in Amman*. London: Quartet Books, 1998.

Nicholson, Reynold. *Translations of Eastern Poetry and Prose*. London: Curzon Press, 1987.

Noonan, John. "Tales of the Hoja." *Saudi Aramco World*. September/October, 1997, p. 30-39.

Nuwayhid, Jamal Salim. *Abu Jameel's Daughter and Other Stories: Arab Folk Tales from Palestine and Lebanon*. Northhampton, MA: Interlink Books, 2002

Pellat, Charles. *The Life and Works of Jahiz*. Berkeley: University of California Press, 1969.

Riordan, James. *Tales from Tartary*. New York: Viking Press, 1978.

Riverbend. *Baghdad Burning: Girl Blog from Iraq*. N.Y.: The Feminist Press, 2005.

Senaveratne, John. *Dictionary of Proverbs of the Sinhalese*. Colombo: Times of Ceylon Co., 1936.

Shepard, Katya. *The Sandal-Wood Box*. Richard Sadler, 1972.

Spagnoli, Cathy. *Asian Tales and Tellers*. Little Rock: August House, 1998.

Thakuru, Hassan. "We say, 'Enough is Enough' ". khttp://www.dhivehiobserver.com/columns/Ha   7 December 2005

The Sayings of Muhammad. New Delhi: Goodword Books, 1997.

Usmah ibn Munqidh. *An Arab-Syrian Gentleman and Warrior in the Period of the Crusades*. Philip K. Hitti, trans. Princeton, N.J.: Princeton University Press, 1987.

Zim, Jacob. *My Shalom, My Peace*. Tel Aviv: Sabra Books, 1975.

Acknowledgements

Grateful acknowlegment is made to the following for permission to reprint previously published material:

The story 'The Wedding Cakes' is from *From the Land of Sheba: Yemeni Folk Tales*, retold by Carolyn Han, translated by Kamal Ali al-Hegri, published by Interlink Books, an imprint of Interlink Publishing Group, Inc. (www.interlinkbooks.com). Text copyright Carolyn Han 2005. Reprinted by permission.

The story 'A Whole Brain' is from *Tales Told in Tents* by Sally Pomme Clayton published by Frances Lincoln Ltd.,   2004. Reproduced by permission of Frances Lincoln Ltd, 4 Torriano Mews, Torriano Avenue, London NW5 2RZ.

For the story 'My Mother, Palestine' by Ramzy Baroud in Holliday, Laurel. *Children of Israel, Children of Palestine*. N.Y.: Pocket Books, 1998.

For the story 'The Ani and the Migoi' by Kunzang Choden from *Folktales of Bhutan*. Bangkok; White Lotus, 1993.

For excerpts from *An Arab Syrian Gentleman and Warrior in the Period of the Crusades* by Usamah ibn Munqidh, translated by Philip K. Hitti. Princeton, N.J.: Princeton University Press, 1987.

For the tale 'The Visit' from *Asian Tales and Tellers* by Cathy Spagnoli. Little Rock; August House, 1998.

For the story, 'Masarasenani dan Matahari' (Masarasenani and The Sun) retold by Murti Bunanta and illustrated by Hardiyono. Published by Kelompok Pencinta Bacaan Anak, first edition February 2006.

When I started this impossible project, I eagerly asked for help from Asian storytellers and writers who had become true friends over the years. I thank them all so very much: their story contributions are a special, valued part of the book. Special gratitude is expressed to the authors below for permission to include the following unpublished stories:

Cynthia Mejia Giudici and her mother, Concolacion, of the U.S./Philippines for 'Growing Up', copyright 2006.

Honda Kazu of Japan for 'The Dark Temple', copyright 2003.

Ly Sieng of U.S./Cambodia for 'Ly Sieng's Journey', copyright 1998.

Mabel Sieh of Hong Kong for 'My Father's Hands', copyright 2003.

Mohd Taib Bin Mohamed of Malaysia for 'Si Luncai', 'Batu Gajah', copyright 2006.

Rosemarie Somaiah of Singapore for 'Kamut's Story', copyright 2006.

Sheila Wee of Singapore for 'Rajah Suran', copyright 2003.

Wajuppa Tossa of Thailand for 'Maeng Nguan', copyright 2003.

All efforts were made to seek permission for printed material used outside of public domain and fair use educational policies. Please accept our apologies and contact the writer if we weren't able to reach you.

The rest of this book is based, in part, on past research in South, Southeast, and East Asia, and with Southeast Asians in the U.S. For that I must thank The Korea Foundation, The Japan Foundation, the U.S. State Department, U.S.I.A., The Korea

Society, the Ministry of Culture in India, Singapore's National Book Development Council, the Washington Commission for the Humanities, the East Asia Center at University of Washington, and all of the organisations that have helped me.

The list of individual tellers, folklore scholars, teachers, writers, and friends who have shared stories and more with me over the last three decades is a very long one. I trust that you know who you are and know that you are very much appreciated. Of course, my wonderful family – my parents, my husband, and our amazing son Manu – are the ones who deserve the most credit for their patience, faith, and constant love.